SHERLOCK HOLMES AND THE LEGEND OF THE GREAT AUK

The Early Casebook of Sherlock Holmes

Book Five

Linda Stratmann

Also in the Early Casebook of Sherlock Holmes
Sherlock Holmes and the Rosetta Stone Mystery
Sherlock Holmes and the Explorers' Club
Sherlock Holmes and the Ebony Idol
Sherlock Holmes and the Persian Slipper

SHERLOCK HOLMES
AND THE LEGEND OF THE
GREAT AUK

Published by Sapere Books.

24 Trafalgar Road, Ilkley, LS29 8HH
United Kingdom

saperebooks.com

Copyright © Linda Stratmann, 2023

Linda Stratmann has asserted her right to be identified as the author of this work.
All rights reserved.

No part of this publication may be reproduced, stored in any retrieval system, or transmitted, in any form, or by any means, electronic, mechanical, photocopying, recording, or otherwise, without the prior written permission of the publishers.
This book is a work of fiction. Names, characters, businesses, organisations, places and events, other than those clearly in the public domain, are either the product of the author's imagination, or are used fictitiously.
Any resemblances to actual persons, living or dead, events or locales are purely coincidental.

ISBN: 978-0-85495-041-6

In memory of the great auk, and other species uncaringly driven to extinction.

From
Memoirs of a Medical Man
by A. Stamford FRCS

1924

CHAPTER ONE

When I first knew Sherlock Holmes, he had yet to inhabit 221b Baker Street, that famous address to which the great, the good and the evil of this world would one day beat a path. We were both students at Barts Medical College, where I was advancing towards my qualification as a surgeon, while Holmes attended lectures in chemistry and anatomy, and conducted his own independent, unsupervised, and often hazardous experiments. His lodgings were in Montague Street, close by the British Museum, where he was often found in the great library, deeply engrossed in scholarly studies of the criminal mind. The museum had good reason to be grateful to Holmes, although his brilliant solution to the Rosetta Stone mystery was not made public at the time, due to the sensitive nature of the event. Once that alarming case was concluded, the museum's directors returned to their everyday business of augmenting and maintaining its prized collections. They also supervised the perpetual rivalry for exhibition space between the antiquities and natural history departments, which were then obliged to share the Bloomsbury building.

My good friend George Luckhurst, who is a scholar of classical Greek sculpture, and knew Holmes from their college days, was then an assistant keeper of the museum's oriental galleries, and thus I was regularly invited to private viewings of new and important acquisitions before the public ever saw them. Holmes rarely showed an interest in these events, but I am about to describe the one occasion on which I was able to engage his earnest attention.

Holmes was in the students' reading room at Barts, where he often repaired to stretch his long frame after a day hunched over a bench in the chemistry laboratory. I found him scouring the daily newspapers for reports of sensational trials and shaking his head with vexation at the singular lack of imagination of the British criminal. I made bold to interrupt his research by suggesting he might like to go to the inaugural viewing of the museum's new attraction in the ornithology department. 'It is a specimen of the great auk, which is generally believed to be extinct,' I said.

'I assume it is dead,' he said drily. 'A living one would be something of a novelty.'

'Stuffed and mounted,' I said, 'and I have been told it now stands in a beautifully constructed display representing its natural habitat. It caused some excitement recently because it was found in the collection of Sir Andrew Caldie, who died last year. It seems he must have kept it a secret, because no-one who dealt with his estate even knew he had it. And of course, next moment museums all over the world started to make bids for it. But they needn't have troubled themselves, because when his will was read it was found that he had left all his collection to the British Museum.'

'How generous,' said Holmes. 'Although I confess that the only stuffed bird which might attract my interest at present is a well roasted fowl.'

'But there is a mystery attached to this one,' I said. I allowed myself a pause. Holmes remained impassive, but his nostrils quivered like those of a hound attracted by a scent. 'There is no record of where and when Sir Andrew acquired it. I am sure it is genuine, as two of the greatest experts in that field, Professor Beare and Dr Woodley have examined it and are satisfied, but all the same, there is an air of secrecy which has resulted in all kinds of rumours, none of which are flattering to any of the parties involved.'

'Rumours so rarely are,' said Holmes. 'Do not regale me with them. I prefer to draw my own conclusions untarnished by another man's bile.' He folded his newspaper and laid it aside. 'I am at your disposal.'

In 1877 the British Museum galleries were open to the public three days a week, and only during the hours of daylight, there being no artificial lighting allowed due to fear of fire. The viewing was to be held during one of the days of closure. The occasion was by ticket only, although Luckhurst was easily able to obtain permission for Holmes and me to be admitted as his guests.

The new exhibit, I was told, had generated considerable anticipation amongst ornithologists since specimens of the great auk were rare and costly, and rarities were always deemed to be more interesting than commoner birds. The last acquisition of a great auk known to have been collected on British shores was bequeathed to the museum in 1819, but since the living bird was then still occasionally seen in northern waters it did not attract more than the usual numbers of visitors. Recent lectures on the subject of extinct birds had excited fresh interest, but the British auk had been temporarily withdrawn from display for necessary conservation work. It was hoped that the announcement in the scientific and public press of the new specimen would increase attendance. Just for a while, the humble bird would rival even the renowned Rosetta Stone.

The afternoon of our visit lay on the cusp of spring and summer, and vivid daylight was streaming through the high windows of the museum as we passed through the lofty

Grecian styled entrance hall. I never failed to appreciate the beauty and subtle colours of this vestibule, which led to the magnificent main staircase. It did seem like a strange contrast, one half of the museum devoted to the most glorious and fascinating art, and the other to stuffed animals, sections of wood, and the grey gloom of fossils and molluscs.

My previous visits to the museum had not included a tour of the bird specimens, and I was astonished to find that this collection occupied almost the whole length of the eastern zoological gallery. I had not until that moment appreciated the enormous extent of the passion amongst naturalists for studying birds, and the fierce determination of collectors and museums to obtain examples of every species. The larger exhibits were displayed in numbered wall cases mounted on both sides of the long room, above which hung scholarly works of art, while adjacent table cases contained eggs and nests as well as smaller birds. I had heard of young men known as 'eggers' who collect birds' eggs, much as some collect stamps or coins. I could understand the charm of the delicate porcelain-like perfection, but I am not sure I would want to risk life and limb climbing trees to deprive innocent creatures of their offspring.

I had brought my copy of the visitors' guide, but it was not hard to see where we were bound. There was a grouping of about twenty persons around those cases which were, so the guide proclaimed, devoted to 'inhabitants of polar regions', and one of the cases was protected by a curtain for the unveiling.

As we arrived, one of the museum assistants who was carrying a bundle of pamphlets handed each of us a copy. Entitled *The Great Auk*, it bore an engraving of the famous bird, and the commentary was jointly authored by Prof R. Owen, Prof L. T. Beare and Dr V. W. Woodley.

Luckhurst, being principally an enthusiast of sculpture, had confided in me that he was more interested in the eggs on display than the birds that had laid them, and it was his amusement to try and detect which were plaster replicas and which the actual specimens.

Most of those assembled for the unveiling were unknown to me, but one gentleman appeared very familiar as I had seen him portrayed in the illustrated journals as a man of distinction. A tall, thin, very stooped figure, leaning upon a twisted and gnarled walking stick, lank wisps of grey hair descending to his shoulders. His face bore a mild expression, but I had heard that while he was kindly to those who supported his views he could, if provoked, turn cruelly upon his adversaries. This was the superintendent of the museum's natural history department, the leading anatomist of his day, the dinosaur man himself, the revered and feared Professor Sir Richard Owen.

CHAPTER TWO

Luckhurst, with the most elaborate courtesy, introduced Holmes and me to Sir Richard, and the two gentlemen experts in the field of ornithology. I could not help but notice that though Holmes had not met any of these worthies, all had heard his name, although the details of his recent services to the museum were not a subject for open discussion. Professor Beare must have been some eighty years of age, but with a bright eye, a firm step, and a cheerful demeanour. We learned that he had long ago been granted the popular soubriquet of 'the collector of penguins' as those birds were his particular passion. His assistant, Dr Woodley, was a sturdy fellow in his middle forties with prematurely thinning hair and a great bush of deep chestnut-coloured beard. During our brief conversation I saw him regard his superior with considerable respect and deference.

'And now, gentlemen, you must excuse me, as it is time for my most pleasurable duty,' said Professor Beare, with a humble little bow as he left us to make the address. He took his place in front of the curtained cabinet, indicating to the assembly by means of a soft cough that the announcement was imminent. As we waited for his words, I was impressed to see that he did not read from notes as so many speakers do, but spoke extempore.

'Miss Caldie,' he began, with a respectful nod in the direction of a serious-looking young lady in steel-framed spectacles, 'our honoured director, distinguished scholars, visitors, and all those who make birds their study, it is my great honour and privilege to unveil only the second example of the great auk acquired by this museum. We must be grateful to the late Sir Andrew Caldie for his generous bequest. Sir Andrew was not simply a notable sportsman, but a dedicated collector, and a skilled preserver of specimens. His book, *The Art of Preserving Birds* has inspired and informed many a youthful naturalist. Our thanks are also due to Mr Caldie and Miss Caldie for their work on their grandfather's estate, which has brought the collection to us in perfect condition.'

Miss Caldie, as befitted the granddaughter of the late Sir Andrew, was a solemnly dignified young lady; however, the deportment of her brother suggested that he was unimpressed both by his surroundings and the event. The remaining members of the gathering were about my age or younger and I guessed were either junior assistants in the museum or students. Two uniformed orderlies stood by the wall opposite to observe the proceedings.

'This new acquisition,' continued the professor, 'will undoubtedly be of great public interest and will add to our knowledge of this bird which, sad to say, is now generally believed to be extinct.' At these last words, Professor Beare paused, and a pained expression bloomed upon his face, the kind of wince I usually associate with a sudden attack of dyspepsia. I thought in this case, however, the eminent gentleman was grieving for the demise of a species. 'I am often accused of being sentimental about bird life,' he went on, 'and I must confess to a personal fondness for the great auk. To those who were fortunate enough to see it alive, on land it appeared awkward, ungainly, almost comical in gait, but the true domain of this noble bird was the sea. There it moved with extraordinary skill and speed in pursuit of the fish which were its diet, and I have been told by fishermen that it could outpace any vessel.'

Recovering his good humour, he continued, 'I am especially delighted to welcome to our gathering Professor Newton of Cambridge University, who will no doubt record this event in his esteemed journal, the *Ibis*, and I also welcome Mr Smith, editor of the *Natural History Review*.'

Professor Newton, who I later learned was a distinguished figure in the world of ornithology, was then approaching fifty, and was rather stout with large side whiskers. I could not help but notice that he walked with a pronounced limp, as one leg appeared to be shorter than the other. Mr Smith was a younger and more slightly built man, who appeared to be anticipating the unveiling with neither pleasure nor excitement. In fact, his expression marked him out for my attention. His forehead was furrowed with concern, and he chewed anxiously on his lower lip. There were little convulsive movements of his fingers, suggesting either some disease or an advanced nervous state. I thought that his mood might have something to do with personal grief since he was wearing a thick black armband and there was a sombre adornment to his hat, indicating a recent bereavement. I glanced at Holmes, who was also observing Smith, and wondered what his conclusions might be.

'And now,' said Professor Beare, pausing with a smile as he surveyed his audience. Mr Caldie had been glancing at his watch, but on a sharp nudge from his sister he reluctantly put it away. The students, who had been in whispered conversation, fell silent and tried to look attentive.

'It only remains,' continued Beare, 'for me to unveil this specimen. Miss Caldie, gentlemen, I now reveal to you *Pinguinus impennis*, the great auk.'

He drew aside the curtain, and amongst the onlookers there was some shuffling forward to gaze upon the bird in the glass case.

The great auk, it has to be admitted, is not a creature of great beauty. It is large, between two and three feet in height, and rather plump. It stands upright on broad webbed feet. The plumage is black at the back and white at the front, arranged very like that of the penguin, which it somewhat resembles, and the wings, if one can call them such, are small and folded tightly by its sides. It is the head that impresses, though, held proudly high, with an oval white patch in front of each eye and a large powerful beak, black delicately barred with white.

The specimen had been mounted on a low plinth of varnished wood. This was partly concealed by expert modelling added by the museum's sculptors, intended to resemble the bird's habitat: grey coastal rocks, and a painted sea tipped with white waves.

One of the students said humorously to another that with a quick burst of galvanism it might be brought back to life.

I could not help but look at Mr Smith's reaction, and his expression of concern had deepened. He now appeared to be angry rather than distressed.

After staring through the glass at the exhibit, he began to tremble and clenched his fists, then he stepped aside and confronted Sir Richard, staring up fearlessly at the much taller man.

'How dare you inflict this fraud upon the public and upon science!' he exclaimed. 'No wonder there is no record of where and when this specimen was collected. This thing is no more than a patchwork assembled to resemble the great auk. Oh, there may be some fragments of a genuine damaged skin included, but there is more of the penguin and the razorbill about it. You, sir, are well known to be a despoiler of other men's work and a barrier to their advancement in order to enhance your own reputation. You are a man who can no longer be trusted, and this abomination has taken place under your direction!'

To his credit, Owen appeared to be wholly unfazed by this damning criticism. Perhaps, I thought, the world of ornithology was more contentious than I had imagined. Lowering his piercing dark gaze upon his furious critic, Owen declared, 'Young man, I must excuse you your foolish declarations, as you have clearly overestimated both your knowledge and your importance.' He then very pointedly turned his back on his accuser.

Undeterred, Smith plunged a hand into his coat and pulled out a small hammer, an action which drew horrified gasps from all present. For one dreadful moment we all thought he was about to rain savage blows on the head of the elderly anatomist, but instead he swung about and made a sudden rush at the glass front of the cabinet which housed the great auk. He raised the hammer and was about to strike when Holmes, with cool presence of mind, intercepted him and seized the hand holding the hammer in such a way as to entirely control its progress. Then, with a movement too rapid for the eye to see, he twisted it from Smith's grasp, eliciting a yelp of pain. Seconds later, Smith was sprawling face down on the floor, with Holmes bending over him, the hammer in one hand and the would-be assailant's wrist held firmly in the other. The two orderlies, both burly fellows, ran up and took charge of the agitated man, who now found himself pinned to the ground, helpless.

'That was smart work,' said Dr Woodley with an exhalation of relief. 'Have you studied abroad?'

'Oh, not so far as that,' said Holmes. 'The art of combat has many branches.' He said no more, but I guessed that our boxing instructor liked to impart, to his most valued students, skills not permitted in the roped ring but very useful outside of it.

'We had better call the police,' said Professor Beare. 'The man is a danger to the public and himself.'

Smith, perhaps satisfied that he had made his point, declined to offer any resistance to his captors, and now that he was not wielding a weapon, he did not appear the slightest bit dangerous.

'If I might say something,' intervened Professor Newton, mildly. 'I believe that Mr Smith is the son of the late Professor Robert Witwer Smith, who died earlier this year under extremely tragic circumstances.' There were gasps from several of those present who must have recognised the name, and their rapid whispers informed others who did not. 'The poor fellow is undoubtedly deranged with grief. Might I suggest that he is simply escorted home to his mother, who can take care of him.'

'Oh,' said Professor Owen, with a slight sneer. '*That* Mr Smith. All now becomes clear. He has been something of a nuisance. Really, he ought not to have been admitted.'

'I must agree with Professor Newton,' said Dr Woodley. 'It would be best to avoid any suggestion of scandal involving the museum. I am sure we are all confident that Smith is mistaken regarding the exhibit, which he has had almost no time to examine, but there will always be those who are jealous of our collections and like to believe the worst.'

Most of us looked to Professor Owen for a final ruling. After a growl of displeasure, he reluctantly agreed. 'But if Smith dares to publish his ridiculous accusations,' he went on, with a ferocious shake of his walking stick, 'he will find himself in court on a criminal charge.' Owen swept a savage gaze over the little assembly. 'And any employee of this museum who breathes one word of this outrage to a person not here present, will be subject to instant dismissal.'

'I can assure you,' said Professor Newton, soothingly, 'that the *Ibis* will be silent on this aspect of the exhibition. In fact, I might delay publication until all controversy is settled. Once Mr Smith is more himself, I will if necessary call upon him and have a friendly word. I hope he will see the error of his ways.'

'That is a very generous offer,' said Professor Beare. 'I do hope that Mr Smith is agreeable to receiving Professor Newton in that spirit.'

Smith, from his prone position, nodded, and was helped to his feet, although the orderlies kept a firm grip on his arms. He spoke only to thank Professor Newton, and not having a suitable card on his person, he provided his address, which was duly noted, after which he was conducted from the gallery. Although much calmer, he was still trembling, and we were relieved to see him go. Owen, with a contemptuous grunt, stumped away to where he said he had important matters to attend to, and Professor Beare called for order and addressed those of us who remained.

'Miss Caldie, gentlemen, I would like to reassure you all that the accusations made by that poor unhappy individual are without foundation, and I trust that not a word of this unfortunate incident will be spoken outside this room.' There was general assent.

Holmes showed the hammer to Professor Newton. 'If I am not mistaken, this is a geological implement,' he said.

'Yes. Mr Smith is only recently returned from New Zealand, where he has spent many years searching for fossil remains of flightless birds. This can be returned to him when we are satisfied that he is well again.'

'I have made a note of his address, and since I reside not far from there, I will undertake that duty,' said Holmes. 'If I remember correctly, there was an inquest reported in the newspapers regarding a Professor Smith last January. I take it that was Mr Smith's unfortunate father. Is there anything I ought to know before I pay a visit?'

Newton hesitated, then beckoned us to a short distance from the throng before he provided further details. 'Yes, it was he,' he confided. 'Mrs Smith had written to her son to advise him that his father was unwell, and he decided to return to London. The incident occurred while he was on the voyage. Professor Smith suffered a brainstorm and assaulted his wife with a razor, then turned it upon himself. Dreadful business.'

Holmes nodded but said nothing.

Miss Caldie arrived at our side like a small but well-trimmed ship. She cannot have been aged more than twenty-five, but her general manner spoke of great assurance. I think she must have been rather pretty, only she made every effort to disguise this, as if there were more weighty matters on her mind. She was very plainly dressed, like a governess, with a simple bonnet devoid of ornament. Her only jewellery was a mourning brooch. The brightest plumage of the family was displayed by her brother, who was some two or three years older, and a devotee of fashion. His only concession to remembrance of his late grandfather was a narrow black ribbon around his hat. He had the swagger of a man who wished us to think he had money to spend.

'Professor Newton,' said Miss Caldie, 'it cannot have escaped your attention that this unfounded accusation does implicate my grandfather. I wish to assure everyone concerned that it would be quite out of his character to commit such an outrage on science.'

Professor Beare had come to join us and addressed Miss Caldie. 'I attach no blame of any kind to your grandfather,' he reassured her.

'I am of the same opinion,' said Newton. 'But is there nothing in his papers to prove where and when he obtained the specimen?'

'I only know he could not have collected it himself, since he never travelled to those parts of the world where the great auk was found,' said Miss Caldie. 'He preferred more tropical climes. He did however purchase interesting specimens from other collectors.'

'I wonder if I might be permitted to examine the exhibit?' asked Holmes.

Newton hesitated. 'What is your area of expertise, if I might be so bold to ask?'

'Observation,' said Holmes, producing his magnifying glass from his pocket.

'I have no objection,' said Professor Beare. 'Mr Holmes is a trustworthy friend of the museum and will of course understand that the exhibit is very fragile.' Dr Woodley had by now joined the conversation and Professor Beare turned to him. 'Woodley, if you would fetch the key to the case?'

Woodley appeared to share Newton's concern, but after a moment he gave a slight nod and went to get the key.

'I promise I will not handle it. I will only take a closer look,' said Holmes.

While we waited, Luckhurst came to speak to us. 'That was nice work, old chap,' he said. 'You have learned a few new tricks since you boxed at college.'

'More than a few,' said Holmes. I said nothing, but I have found over the years that Holmes never lost the ability to astonish both me and others with his knowledge and skills, some of a curiously esoteric nature. When one is fighting for one's life, there is no room for nicety.

Woodley returned to unlock the case, then watched anxiously as Holmes stepped forward and leaning in closely, gazed through the searching lens as it travelled over the curious bird. After some minutes Holmes said, 'There is reason to suggest that this exhibit was not prepared from an intact skin. It might have been damaged when collected or more likely imperfectly preserved before it was assembled. There are clear signs of repairs having been done but that would not, I assume, be unusual in the circumstances?'

'Not at all,' said Beare. 'In fact, I might suggest that that was what led poor Smith to his misguided conclusion. He is an expert in fossils, not the art of preserving animal skins.'

Holmes bent down further, folding his long thin frame to study the wooden plinth on which the bird stood. 'There is no inscription, which I would have expected,' he said, 'either in Latin or English.'

'The great auk has had many names,' said Beare. 'I have even known it to be called the northern penguin, although it is not related to the penguin, which is only found in the southern hemisphere.'

'I would be obliged if the exhibit could be lifted sufficiently to allow me to fully examine the base,' said Holmes.

Beare nodded to Woodley, who donned his gloves and with great care brought the bird closer to Holmes's view, raising it slightly as he did so. Holmes scanned the full circumference of the base with his glass, and then unexpectedly knelt down and studied the underside. He stood up. 'There was once a label pasted to the base,' he said, 'but it has been removed.'

'Oh,' exclaimed Beare, 'I do believe I did not notice that. Perhaps the seller or manufacturer's label was once there?'

'But why remove it?' asked Holmes.

'Perhaps,' offered Miss Caldie, 'my grandfather used a base which had previously been intended for a different bird and removed the old label.'

'Without replacing it?' said Holmes.

No-one had any further theories to offer. Woodley carefully repositioned the exhibit in its case and once it was safely in place, he locked the door with noticeable relief.

As we left, I waited for Holmes to reveal his conclusions about the exhibit, but he said nothing on that subject. 'I think an interview with Mr Smith might prove to be instructive,' he said. 'But it is very clear to me that more than one person who was present at that event is keeping a secret.'

CHAPTER THREE

Holmes decided not to visit Mr Smith unannounced in view of that gentleman's unpredictable state of anxiety. He sent a brief note merely to inform Smith that he had the little hammer in his possession and would gladly return it if he could be allowed to pay a call. While waiting for a response, he made discreet enquiries at the museum. Holmes particularly wished to discover the origins of Smith's fury against Professor Owen. There was something in Smith's manner which had suggested to him that there might be personal as well as professional reasons.

His enquiries elicited facts which he later shared with me. The young editor of the *Natural History Review* had for some years been curator of fossils at a museum in New Zealand. He had a special interest in the extinct moa, reputedly the largest bird that ever lived. It was Professor Owen who had first identified and described this bird from bones that had been sent to him. Owen consequently regarded himself as the supreme authority on the moa, although he had never visited New Zealand. Smith, with his fifteen years of field study, was eager to challenge that claim.

The disgruntled curator's full name was Charles Witwer Smith. His father, Professor Robert Witwer Smith, had been an anatomist whose stature in the discipline had once rivalled that of Professor Owen. The two men had not been on friendly terms. Professor Smith had alleged that Owen had used his influence to prevent him from publishing papers and examining important specimens, and had then appropriated his discoveries and conclusions, claiming them as his own. All efforts to prove these allegations had failed, but the damage was done. The older Smith's star had faded, and he had struggled with despondency.

Long before Holmes hung out his shingle as a consulting detective, he had begun compiling the commonplace books in which he would store the notes and extracts of newspapers which would, in later years, exasperate Watson with their bulk and untidiness. One article Holmes had not included in his collection recorded the inquest on Professor Robert Witwer Smith, which, although he did not say so, I believe he took as a lesson to neglect nothing that might one day prove to be of interest. He was obliged to locate it in the British Museum library's newspaper collection, regaling me afterwards with the distressing details.

Professor and Mrs Smith were living in a pleasant villa, which they had first occupied in more affluent times. It was one of a row of six in a quiet location, the respectable neighbours wholly unfamiliar with scenes of violent crime. The drama began at the breakfast table one morning while the Smiths' only servant was on an errand to fetch milk. There had been no-one else in the house at the time. Their immediate neighbour, a Mrs Bailey, had been alerted by screams of 'Help! Murder!' coming from next door. She hurried out into the street but was understandably reluctant to go and see what the matter was and sent her maid to alert a policeman. At that moment, Samuel Hepden, a young coal merchant's carrier who made regular deliveries in that area, was approaching on his cart. Mrs Bailey begged him to go and help, and he obligingly jumped down and tried to enter the house by the front door. Failing to do so, he broke a window and climbed in. There were more loud shrieks from Mrs Smith, which subsided into anguished sobs. Mrs Bailey waited outside, then Hepden appeared at the window and told her to fetch a doctor.

The home and surgery of Dr Scales was nearby, and Mrs Bailey demanded he come at once as there was murder being done. At the Smiths' house Scales found a room liberally spattered with blood. Mrs Smith was alive, but her hands and arms had been slashed with a razor as she tried to defend herself. Her husband was dead. After attacking her, he had cut his own throat.

The coroner was informed that Professor Smith had not been under the influence of any drug or alcohol and was therefore fully conscious and active until the moment of his death.

A heavily bandaged Mrs Smith told the inquest that her husband had been increasingly melancholy in recent years, and she had been afraid for some time that he might lay violent hands upon himself. That morning, something he read in a scientific journal had sent him into a rage, and when she tried to soothe him, he had pulled a razor from his pocket and attacked her. Only the wildness of his movements had prevented her injuries from being any worse. When her rescuer burst in, her husband had applied the razor to his own throat. The verdict was that Professor Smith had taken his own life.

A back number of the *Illustrated Police News* completed the story. The artist had been prolific, providing an engraving of the late professor and his widow, and a dramatic impression of the awful scene in the breakfast room. The coal man, Samuel Hepden, had obligingly posed for a sketch holding a coal sack in one hand and an iron sack hook in the other, in front of the broken window of the villa. He was hailed a hero for risking his life in the rescue. Young ladies wrote him letters proposing marriage, and a police inspector said he was just the kind of fellow he wanted on the force.

Two days after the scene in the museum, Holmes received a note from Professor Beare, asking to meet him at the museum on an urgent matter. 'And so, at last, the secrets emerge,' said Holmes. 'You might as well come, too, Stamford, if you have the time.'

I did not have the time, but I agreed to come in any case. A casual suggestion from Holmes always seemed to act upon me as a demand impossible to refuse.

On our arrival we were greeted by Professor Beare and Dr Woodley. The cheerfulness and optimism of the two eminent ornithologists which we had seen at the unveiling of the great auk was absent, their manner and voices suggesting that their business was not of a pleasant nature. They conducted us to a private office much adorned with portraits of their avian friends. Penguins especially featured. I admit that I began to see the fascination with these curious birds. From a distance a waddle of penguins resemble a gathering of formally clad gentlemen, waving their little flipper-like wings as if gesticulating in debate. Some species even had head feathers like quizzically raised bushy eyebrows, which reminded me of one of my professors at Barts.

As soon as we took our seats Dr Woodley made sure to close the door very firmly, as if that precaution was sufficient to exclude all others. I had a strong feeling that the distinguished co-author of the recent pamphlet was not to be present at our meeting and probably knew nothing about it.

Professor Beare presided. 'Gentlemen,' he began, 'I address you now as you are known to be friends of the museum, and have rendered valuable service in the past, for which we are very grateful. Not only that, but we have complete trust that you will respect our confidence. Before I start, I would like you to reassure us that no word of this meeting will be spoken outside of this room.'

'With the caveat that we cannot agree to conceal a crime, you may rely on our strict secrecy,' said Holmes.

'Oh!' exclaimed Beare, startled at the suggestion. 'I do not ask you to conceal any illegality, rather I wish you be complicit in my efforts to prevent a terrible act to the detriment of science.'

'Then I agree wholeheartedly,' said Holmes, and I too nodded assent.

Professor Beare drew a deep breath to steady himself before he commenced. 'I am sorry to say that I received a visit this morning from a correspondent of the *Pall Mall Gazette*. To my horror, he appeared to be furnished with the full details of what occurred at the unveiling of our exhibit of the great auk. Not only the dreadful action of Mr Smith, which is quite bad enough, but his wholly unwarranted accusations of fraud which can only serve to bring the museum into disrepute. This person actually had the effrontery to ask me if Smith's attack was some kind of theatrical performance, a tawdry masquerade arranged by the museum to draw attention to the exhibit and increase numbers of visitors, a suggestion as disgraceful as it is untrue. All I could tell him was that Mr Smith was clearly overwrought and I had no doubt that he now regretted his outburst. I suggested very strongly that the *Gazette* should not publish an account of the event, but he advised me that it was pointless to ask as he had been told it would appear in the London evening newspapers today and then the dailies tomorrow morning, and as you know, the papers all over the kingdom are wont to take their copy from London. He believed that the *Illustrated Police News* is already preparing a front-page portrait impression of the incident. It is a catastrophe!'

'Indeed,' agreed Dr Woodley, solemnly. 'Professor Owen would be especially troubled by this, as it throws into confusion his long-cherished scheme for a separate museum devoted to natural history, the construction of which is still far from completion. We are all very anxious for that to open, as we would like to be able to display our collection to the best advantage and I know the antiquities department would be delighted to see the removal of the whales. When I last spoke to Sir Richard, he was determined to have Smith accused of slander. We have been trying to calm him, as an appearance in court might only provoke further accusations and more scandals. For all we know the newspapers might have been questioning Smith, and who knows what he is saying?' He threw up his hands in a gesture of despair. Even through the bush of beard his concern at the gravity of the situation was very apparent.

'I think the papers will hesitate to publish obvious libels,' said Beare, 'but all the same, the slightest breath of unprofessional behaviour could damage us dreadfully, and you know how we rely on our annual grant of funds from Parliament. An accusation of this kind could cost us dearly.'

'I appreciate and sympathise with your difficulties,' said Holmes. 'Do you wish me to discover who revealed the incident to the press? I should mention that there is a natural reluctance amongst pressmen to expose the identity of their informants without financial persuasion. But even if I were to learn the name, it would avail you nothing since the facts of the matter, the attack and the allegations, even if they are mistaken, really did occur.'

'It must be Smith,' declared Professor Beare. 'Every other individual present gave a solemn promise to say nothing. No employee of the museum would do such a thing, and Mr and Miss Caldie would hardly expose their grandfather to an accusation of fraud.'

'We cannot prevent the publicity you will receive today,' said Holmes. 'In fact, I fear that if we were to make any further attempt to silence the press or witnesses, it might only increase speculation and make matters worse.'

Beare gave a little sorrowful groan, but he clearly accepted Holmes's analysis. 'Then what can we do?'

'I assume, gentlemen, that you have no shred of doubt that the exhibit is genuine, or you would never have permitted it to be displayed?' said Holmes.

'None whatsoever,' said Professor Beare, firmly. 'Mr Smith appeared in his tirade to be implying that what we had was the body of a penguin and the beak of a razorbill, which is a nonsense. I very much doubt that he has made a detailed study of the great auk, or he would not have made such an error. The shape of the vestigial wings and structure of the plumage are quite different.'

'I entirely agree,' said Woodley, with equal firmness.

'You are confident that a partial skin of a great auk has not been repaired with that of another bird?'

At this, Beare showed a slight hesitation, then straightened his shoulders with a determined effort. 'I am,' he declared. His associate nodded emphatic agreement.

'Then,' Holmes continued, 'I suggest that your best course of action would be to arrange for an independent expert examination of the exhibit and prove beyond any doubt that the accusations of fraud are incorrect. You should make sure to advise the press that this is being done, and once it is complete you may publish the results. You might even invite a representative of the press to witness the procedure. You should also consider labelling the exhibit to make the provenance clearer. It would be educational for the public to know more about the handling and restoration of such an item, and create even more interest in the display. Then when Smith recovers his equilibrium, he might be persuaded to quietly withdraw his accusation.'

'Is there anyone we would trust to carry out such an examination?' asked Professor Beare, turning to his associate.

'The exhibit is quite delicate, and we would not want it to be damaged,' said Woodley.

'Surely you would be prepared to trust Ward and Co. of Piccadilly, who carry out the taxidermy work for the museum,' said Holmes. 'And any slight harm that might befall the exhibit must be a small price to pay for restoring the reputation of the collection.' There was a silence as Beare and Woodley considered Holmes's words, then they glanced at each other. 'If that is all you wished to ask me,' said Holmes, 'then I shall take my leave.' He rose to his feet, and I did the same. 'What a shame it is that we were unable to see the label that was removed from the base of the exhibit,' he said. 'That might have told us a great deal. As a matter of curiosity, gentlemen, why did you remove it, and what did it reveal?'

The reaction to Holmes's question was a shocked silence. Holmes waited but said nothing more.

'Please sit down, Mr Holmes,' said Professor Beare at last. 'I can see that it is useless to hide anything from you. I will tell you what you need to know, but I am sure you will appreciate the harm it will do if anyone else was to learn of it.' He glanced at me.

'You may trust my associate,' said Holmes. We both sat down.

'Yes, I did remove the label,' admitted Beare. 'I have it safe, but apart from myself only Dr Woodley has seen it. In fact, I do not believe Mr and Miss Caldie ever saw it. The label revealed two things: the place and the date. It read, "Great Auk. St Kilda, 1855".'

'And this signifies the place where the specimen was collected and the year?' Holmes asked.

'That is customary, yes,' said Beare. He then gave a significant pause, so much so that we could only watch as a series of undefinable emotions passed across his face. When he continued, it was more in the manner of a lecture. 'The literature of the great auk shows that the last known specimens to be collected were a breeding pair in Iceland, in 1844. There have been a few reported sightings since, all of them before 1855, none of which have been positively confirmed. The razorbill, which is also known as the lesser auk, is of similar enough appearance that it might be mistaken for the great auk when seen in the water at a distance.'

'There was once a small colony of the great auk which used the island of St Kilda as their annual breeding ground, but none have been seen there for very many years,' added Woodley.

'So what you are saying is that if the date on the label is correct, it means that the bird became extinct more recently than is commonly believed?' asked Holmes. 'Forgive me, gentlemen, but while I appreciate that the precise year of its extinction is of scientific interest, I cannot see why it should be of such a sensitive nature.'

'If indeed the great auk *is* actually extinct,' said Beare, and there was a note of challenge in his voice. 'You must understand me, Mr Holmes,' he continued. 'Not so many years ago, in fact in living memory, there were colonies of the great auk in Icelandic waters and off the coast of Newfoundland and when they came on shore to breed, they numbered in many thousands. Then for reasons which we have yet to fully appreciate, their numbers dwindled and they seemed about to disappear altogether. On one little island, nowadays known as Funk Island, great hosts of seabirds of all kinds came annually to breed, including the great auk. But when a naturalist went to visit the island in 1841 to make a study, he was shocked to find no trace of the live birds he had heard about, only a wilderness of scattered bones.

'Once it became known that there were so very few remaining, the collectors and museums naturally became interested, and they all wanted specimens. It was a collector who ordered the killing of the last two ever seen in Iceland. But many of us stayed hopeful — I certainly did — that somewhere, perhaps in far northern climes, there were places where man did not go and where colonies still thrived. I can tell you now that the esteemed Professor Newton also entertains such hopes. Years have passed and those hopes have not been realised. Not yet. But there are still places unfriendly to man, uninhabited and unexplored, where a creature protected from the extreme cold by its feathers and fat may happily live and breed. And now, with this specimen, my hopes have been raised once more.'

The elderly professor was clearly engaged by a powerful emotion, and both Holmes and I respectfully remained silent. Holmes glanced at Dr Woodley, who obliged us by continuing.

'We do not think there is a colony remaining on St Kilda, since the island is small and populated,' he said. 'If any remained, they would surely have been seen, but we have received no reports. The auk, however, is a powerful swimmer and we think ours might have strayed from another, unpopulated island, where others may still come in substantial numbers every year to lay their eggs.'

'The great auk is better than some people,' said Beare, sadly. 'They mate for life; they stay faithful. If one of a pair should die, the other does not take another mate. This one might have suffered such a loss.'

Woodley said nothing, but his eyes appeared almost tearful. I wondered if the fate of the auk mirrored something in his own life. I dared not ask.

'But we do not wish to attract attention to the region,' said Beare. 'We must not. And for that reason, we have determined not to go there for the time being. If there is such a colony in existence, it must at all costs be protected from the collectors. We have more than enough skins and bones for the purposes of study. Professor Owen wrote a paper on the skeleton of the great auk which will never be bettered. What we ultimately want is to be able to observe the living birds in their native habitats. Let them thrive, let them multiply. Perhaps one day, if they revive in sufficient numbers, we may establish a vivarium at the zoological gardens, where they may live and feed and swim and lay their eggs. That is why at present the place and the date must be kept a secret. There must be no expeditions, no enquiries.'

Holmes was thoughtful. 'Is there any possibility that if you submitted the specimen to Ward and Co., they would be able to deduce from their examination the date and the location where it was collected?'

'An external examination would not be conclusive,' said Beare. 'We have not probed the interior; it is far too fragile. The museum has done no more than gently clean the outer portions. But it is not beyond possibility that whoever collected it left some kind of label or marking inside. And while Ward and Co. are a highly reputable firm, you have seen for yourselves what has happened before a small group of persons whom we believed we could trust. I do not wish to take the risk.'

'What the examination might also show is whether the skin is a whole one, and therefore what it appears to be, or as Mr Smith suggested, a composite of other birds,' Holmes commented.

'We have no doubts that it is genuine,' said Woodley. 'We have no fear in that respect.'

'How would it have been collected?' asked Holmes. 'I saw no evidence of damage from being shot.'

'Ah, well, being a flightless bird, there is no need to shoot them,' said Woodley. 'They were rapid swimmers, but they do not move very fast on land and may be taken by clubbing or throttling, which is less harmful to the skin.'

'I see.' Holmes allowed some moments for thought, tilting his head back and steepling his fingertips. 'What do you wish me to do?'

'I have been told,' said Professor Beare, 'that you can solve the most complicated mysteries that baffle other men. Mr Holmes, I would like you to discover the origins of our specimen and prove it to be genuine, without damaging it or exposing the whole species to the depredations of the collectors. It is not only the reputation of the museum that is at stake. Somewhere, perhaps in these very islands of Britain, I do believe that the great auk is still alive!'

With some reservations Holmes agreed to do what he could. As we left the museum, I asked, 'How did you know that they removed the label?' He gave a wry smile. 'I didn't.'

CHAPTER FOUR

I will not reproduce here all the many accounts of the unfortunate scene at the museum which appeared in the press over the next few days, but I think these contrasting examples will show just how the popular newspapers viewed the event. It was with some relief that we saw that the *Illustrated Police News* did not think an attack on a stuffed bird worthy of a front-page engraving, and it confined its report to an inside column.

The Times

EXTRAORDINARY SCENE IN THE BRITISH MUSEUM

A visitor to the museum who must remain nameless has attempted to destroy an exhibit, the newly unveiled example of the great auk, a flightless bird which is believed to be extinct. It appears that he was under the impression that the specimen was a fraud, despite the fact that it had been determined to be genuine by the museum's experts, including one of the foremost ornithologists in the land, Professor Louis Beare. Fortunately, no harm was done and the assailant, who was in a somewhat nervous state, was conducted away. It is understood that no charges are to be made.

London Morning News

A FOWL DEED

A little bird has sung in my ear with a curious tale. Could my informant be the legendary great auk, of which no living example has been seen in many a year? I doubt it, but it was the subject of a most unusual ruffling of feathers at the British Museum. A gentleman who was recently borne in by the winds from the antipodes, where the cry is 'moa bones! moa bones!' warbled a strange speech in which he accused the museum of foisting an addled specimen of the flightless waddler upon the public. He then attempted to prove his point by committing an assault upon the object of his ire but was snared before he could do so. Who is this man? Is he an expert or a bad egg? Will he be caged? This correspondent would very much like to know.

Sporting Gazette

We continue our series of 'Great Sportsmen of England, Scotland and Wales', with a timely tribute to the late Sir Andrew Caldie. His prowess with the gun was unrivalled, his energy in the pursuit of specimens was admirable, but most of all, even when age and gout limited his endeavours, he remained dedicated to the preservation of his collection. The birds he sought were not to him mere trophies to be displayed, but articles of study which he collected with the utmost care. The result was a treasury of great beauty and scientific interest which he generously bequeathed to the British Museum. One may imagine the shock to those of us who knew Sir Andrew, and most especially to his family, when at the unveiling of his specimen of the great auk, it was denounced to all present as a fraud, assembled from fragments of other birds. This scandalous slander of a great man should be retracted immediately, and we hope to hear very soon that this has taken place.

Holmes later told me that when he next visited the museum, he found that the suspect great auk had been removed from display, and the older specimen restored in its place. 'We thought it best to avoid controversy,' said Dr Woodley, who came to speak with him as he studied the more venerable example. 'Most of our visitors are perfectly happy as long as they see a great auk, and few will even realise it is not the one that has been featured in the newspapers. Young persons like to stand and stare at it to see if they can solve the mystery, when there is none to solve. This one came from Papa Westray in the Orkneys some sixty years ago, and is without a doubt entire and genuine.'

'I rather think the whole affair will be but a brief wonder,' said Holmes. 'In fact, the less we respond to the criticism the better.'

'I agree,' said Woodley without hesitation. 'Naturally I do like to accede to Professor Beare's wishes, as he is a thoroughly worthy man and due the greatest respect. He has been my advisor and mentor for many years. I lost my parents when I was very young, and he has been as a second father to me. He was a tireless force for good during the debate in Parliament which led to the passing of the Act to protect seabirds from wanton destruction. I was honoured to collaborate with him on that work. But — and I would not say it to his face, though I know he is wise enough to suspect the truth — I personally do not think there are great auks alive still. Yes, Professor Newton is still hopeful, but he is one of the few that remain so. The idea of large colonies in the far north was once widely held, but no longer. And the label, which Professor Beare keeps close and studies — I think it could as well read 1835 as 1855. In fact, when I first saw it, I thought 1835 was far more likely, given the dates of the few sightings there have been there. The 1855 could have been a mistake or a slip of the pen. But —' he uttered a soft sigh, and a stroke of his beard revealed an affectionate smile — 'I like to allow the professor his hopes, his dreams. Why not? They are harmless enough. They make him happy.'

'Might I see this label?' asked Holmes.

Woodley took a little time to answer. 'He has not agreed to show it to anyone else. However, if it helps your enquiries — very well, I will ask him if it could be produced. But whatever the date may be, it might mean anything, such as when the specimen was purchased. It proves nothing.'

During this visit Holmes took the opportunity to study the exhibit of the lesser auk, or razorbill, *Alca torda*. As he later observed to me, he entirely agreed with Dr Woodley that while much smaller than its extinct cousin, this bird, if seen in the water from afar, could easily be mistaken for the great auk, as its coloration and beak were very similar. The error would only become apparent when it spread its wings and took flight.

'How interesting,' said Holmes to me the next day, as he perused a letter which had reached him at Bart's Medical College. 'Take a look, Stamford, and tell me what you make of it.'

The letter was a reply to the note he had written to Charles Witwer Smith.

Dear Mr Holmes,

Thank you for your kind note regarding the hammer. I presume you are the gentleman who so expertly removed it from my grasp, thus preventing me from making even more of a spectacle of myself than I had already. For that I am duly grateful.

I will not discuss the recent press notices which tend to suggest that I am subject to delusions. I am sure it pleases Professor Owen to think so. I admit that I was greatly overwrought, and for a brief moment, not fully my own master. I have tried on many occasions to obtain some acknowledgement from Professor Owen of the services my poor late father performed for science. In particular, I have requested that the important fossils he donated to the museum be properly labelled with his name, but my entreaties have been met with silence.

I did not attend the unveiling of Sir Andrew Caldie's bequest with the intention of making a scene, and the little hammer is always in my pocket much as another man might carry a pen or a pipe. But when I saw the bird and the amateurish efforts to render its form, I was appalled that such an object should be foisted on the public. I am not a great expert on the northern flightless birds, but I have made an extensive study of the penguin, both living and in fossil form. The distinguished gentlemen of the museum may have been taken in not so much by the artifice of the taxidermist but their own wishful thinking. Having said that, I have other, more worrying suspicions regarding an individual who I will not name in this letter.

But you will be relieved to know that I have decided for the time being to put those matters behind me for the sake of my family. My unhappy mother has endured so much, and her nerves are very frail. My father's death left her with almost nothing, and she has been obliged to consider taking in lodgers for which she is ill-suited. My intention is now to settle my affairs in this country and return to New Zealand with my mother, and there we will make a pleasant and comfortable life for ourselves. My work on the fossil remains of the moa will continue.

On the subject of the provenance of the great auk, if you care to call upon us next Saturday at four o'clock, I will be happy to enlighten you further.

Yours faithfully
Charles Witwer Smith

'It is a very sensible letter,' I said. 'He admits to a moment of passion which he now regrets and has provided an explanation. Whatever the concerns for his sanity after what occurred, I think they can now be put aside.'

'I look forward to hearing the enlightenment he offers,' said Holmes. 'He has more to tell us, observations he will not put in writing, which therefore must be of a highly sensitive nature. Whether there is any substance to them, is a matter of conjecture.'

'Do you think it was he who spoke to the press?' I asked. 'He does not approve of their sentiments, but he might have given them the bare facts.'

'The museum certainly believes so, and I can understand why. His decision to return to New Zealand does support that supposition, as it removes him from the heat of the debate, but he is far from being the only candidate.'

Holmes wrote a reply to Smith accepting the invitation. Little did we know that it was a meeting which would never take place.

On the day before the proposed meeting, we were in the students' reading room when a porter handed Holmes a letter.

Dear Mr Holmes,

Please forgive me for opening the letter you sent to my son, Charles Witwer Smith, but I did so in the hopes of receiving some news which would help me find him. Would you be kind enough to let me know if you have seen him since Wednesday? After he wrote his letter to you, he went out to attend to some business matters, and I have not seen or heard from him since. This is quite out of character, and I am afraid he may have suffered an accident or been taken ill. I have been everywhere looking for him, but no-one has seen him apart from Mr Selby of the Natural History Review *who spoke to him that afternoon, when he seemed in good spirits and was making plans for the future.*

P. Smith (Mrs)

Holmes started in alarm, thrust the paper into his pocket, fetched his hat and coat and went out without another word. He didn't order me to go with him. He didn't need to.

CHAPTER FIVE

Our way lay north in the direction of Islington, and Holmes did not hesitate to signal to a hansom to convey us there. In later years when expense was not a concern, this was always his preferred mode of transport, a small, fast vehicle which could easily weave its way through the busy traffic of London thoroughfares. It conveyed only two occupants, the better for a private conversation with a trusted associate regarding the investigation which occupied his mind.

'I hope nothing serious has occurred,' I ventured.

'When a man who has made many enemies suddenly vanishes, it is a matter for serious consideration,' said Holmes. 'Two days without a word from a son who was clearly making plans to care for his widowed mother.'

We alighted in a quiet, narrow street, one side of a small square of residential properties which was select without being fashionable or ostentatious. Charles Smith's address was one of a terrace of neat villas, six in number, all smartly painted. They faced a small but well-kept public garden, where paths wound their way around flower beds filled with spring colour, and there were benches thoughtfully placed for enjoying the shade provided by blossom-laden trees.

Holmes took a moment or two to survey the properties and their surroundings. Whatever he learned by doing so, he did not communicate, but strode to the first house on the terrace, Park Villa, and knocked at the door. I had read the accounts of the death of Professor Smith, but even so I was surprised to see that the windowpane, the one through which Mrs Smith's rescuer had burst, had not yet been repaired, but was still boarded up, even though the tragedy had occurred almost three months previously. The work had been done quite roughly from the outside, in the manner of a temporary arrangement simply to secure the property before proper repairs could be made. There was no answer to Holmes's knock, although after about a minute a lace curtain that covered a narrow window by the front door was twitched aside, and we saw the hint of a face. We waited but no-one answered the knock. Holmes tried again. This time the curtain did not move.

I was wondering what to do for the best, when the door of the next house, Walnut Villa, opened, and a maid appeared.

'Excuse me, sirs,' she said politely, 'but I don't believe Mrs Smith is at home. She has gone away in a hurry.'

'That is a pity,' said Holmes, 'as I have a letter from Mrs Smith asking for my help with a serious matter. I believe there is a person in the house, but I have not been admitted.'

The maid, not anticipating this development, wavered indecisively, but at that moment a lady joined her at the door and peered out at us. She was a dainty individual in her middle years, crisply and neatly clad, her hair in pearl-grey curls clustering under a lace cap. 'Gentlemen, I could not help hearing that you wish to see Mrs Smith, but she is not at home, and her maid has been told not to admit strangers without permission.'

'I am sorry about that,' said Holmes, 'as I have come in response to a letter from Mrs Smith concerning her son.'

'Oh?' The lady stepped a little further forward. 'Do you have any news of him?'

'None, I am afraid, but Mrs Smith appealed to me for my help, and I have come to see if I can be of service.' Holmes produced the letter and handed it to the lady.

'Ah yes,' she said, when she had finished perusing it. 'Are you a friend of Mr Smith?'

'I have met him once at the British Museum,' said Holmes. 'He left an item of his property behind, and I wrote to him to say that I had it safe and wished to return it. He replied asking me to pay a visit this coming Saturday. I am a student of anatomy at Barts Medical College, and this is my associate, Mr Stamford, who is undertaking courses in surgery.'

The lady looked at us carefully as if to detect anything in our appearance that might contradict that statement. Satisfied, she returned the letter and said, 'I am Mrs Horace Bailey. I am not sure if anyone can help poor Mrs Smith now. Two policemen came to the house this morning to see her, and she went away with them looking very upset.'

'I am at her command, if need be,' said Holmes, gallantly.

'Oh, well, that is so very kind of you, especially after — I mean, she has few friends, and apart from her son who has been abroad for so very long, she has no close family apart from a widowed sister.' Mrs Bailey hesitated. 'Would you like to come in and wait for her? I was about to have my morning coffee.'

We thanked her and were ushered into a very comfortable property, exquisitely tidy, warm, and well furnished. In the parlour, an elderly lady, her face almost hidden from view by a frilled cap, was settled deeply in an armchair which stood beside the fire and enclosed her like an extra-large garment. Her prominently knuckled hands were busy with some yarn work. Mrs Bailey introduced us to the lady, who was her aunt Jane. We received only a grunt of acknowledgement. I suspected she might be hard of hearing.

The mantelshelf displayed an arrangement of chinaware, all with the shine of recent cleaning, and there was a framed photographic portrait of the lady of the house with her husband, who looked like a bulky wrestler in a tight suit, and two adult sons and a daughter, all of whom had a marked resemblance to their father. Mrs Bailey rang for the maid and gave orders for coffee. 'How long have the Smith family been your neighbours?' asked Holmes as we seated ourselves at a table draped in a fringed velvet cloth that might have done service as a lady's mantle at the opera.

'They came here the same year as we all did, 1861,' said Mrs Bailey. 'That was when the villas were built, and the leaseholds sold. Such an excellent security for us and the children.'

'It is very pleasant and quiet here,' said Holmes.

'Yes,' said Mrs Bailey. 'I — Mr Holmes — you might be able to enlighten me — there were reports in several newspapers about a disturbance in the British Museum, and mention was made of it being caused by a man from the antipodes. I didn't like to ask, but I don't suppose that could have had anything to do with young Mr Smith?'

'I am sorry to say it did,' said Holmes, 'although even the most reliable papers are subject to errors of interpretation. There was an academic disagreement, at which I was present, and yes, Mr Smith expressed his views rather forcefully. It was necessary to calm him down.'

'Ah,' said Mrs Bailey. 'Gentlemen can get so overwrought sometimes. It is a point of honour. They dislike being wrong about anything. If that was his state of mind when he left here, I fear he may have done something to disgrace himself and caused his poor mother even more pain.' She paused. 'I suppose you know about his father?'

'It was in the newspapers,' said Holmes.

The maid arrived with the coffee, which gave us the opportunity of contemplating that dreadful subject while the cups were being filled.

'So unexpected,' said Mrs Bailey, once the maid had departed. 'I knew that Professor Smith had been despondent about his reduced fortunes, but I never thought of him as a man of violence. I suppose one never does with scholarly gentlemen. When they first came to live here, I was told that he was quite the coming man in his field — zoology, I believe. But then he failed to go on as expected; in fact, his students at the university became fewer and fewer. I heard that he had had a disagreement with another man over that book by Mr Darwin, the one that shocked everyone so much, and it was the other man who prevailed and whose views became fashionable. The professor thought that obstacles had been deliberately put in his way to prevent his advancement. Whether that was true or just his fancy, I don't know. Mrs Smith was very worried about him; she even thought that if he became any worse, he might do what he did. Not that he ever threatened to, although — I cannot help wondering…'

We waited for her to continue. No-one knew better than Holmes that people could not endure a silence for long. Mrs Bailey sipped her coffee. We continued to wait.

'I wondered,' she said, 'if Professor Smith ever anticipated what he might be capable of, what he might do if he lost all hope, and made plans accordingly. Mrs Smith once told me that he never trusted insurance companies. He used to say that insurers took your money and then found some excuse not to pay when the time came. Consequently, he was not insured, which turned out to be a favourable thing under the circumstances, as the premiums would have been paid out in vain. He said he preferred a more certain investment and had been assembling a large collection of fossils, presumably with that in mind. That does not sound very valuable to me, but then I know nothing of the subject, and neither does Mrs Smith. I suppose Mr Charles can advise. In any case, they are his now.'

'You saw nothing of the actual incident in which Professor Smith died?' asked Holmes.

Mrs Bailey put down her coffee cup. I sensed that we were about to hear a tale she had told before. 'No, well, I dared not go in. My husband had gone to his office at his usual hour, and there was only myself, Aunt Jane, the cook and the maid. When we heard Mrs Smith cry out, we were not about to intervene for we were in fear of our lives. I sent the maid for a policeman, but then thankfully the coal man came by on his usual round. I said, "Oh, please help Mrs Smith! There is murder being done." And he jumped down from the cart quick as anything and broke in through a window.' Mrs Bailey imitated the action with a tiny fist.

'It is not an easy thing to break a window,' I observed. 'I am sure I would cut myself if I tried it.'

Mrs Bailey gave me the kind of indulgent smile I often receive from motherly ladies. 'Oh, he is very resourceful. He put a coal sack against the glass, and then he struck it with something. A piece of iron from the cart. I don't think he was hurt.

'But then — I heard such shrieks from Mrs Smith, the like of which I never want to hear again. I heard afterwards that that was when the professor made away with himself. Then it all went quiet, apart from Mrs Smith sobbing, and the coal man looked out of the window and said to fetch a doctor. I ran up the road as fast as I could go, because the cook is too stout nowadays to run, and Dr Scales came right away. The coal man said only the doctor must come in, as it was no scene for ladies. He had blood on his clothes.'

'How did Dr Scales enter the house?' asked Holmes. 'The newspapers said the Smiths' maid was on an errand to fetch milk. Was there anyone there to admit him?'

'No, he had to climb through the window as well.'

'When did you next see Mrs Smith?'

'At the inquest. I was so relieved when I heard that young Mr Smith was already on his way home. I knew he would look after her.'

As Mrs Bailey spoke, there was the sound of a carriage outside and she rose and went to the window, carefully parting the curtains the smallest amount possible. 'She is home,' she said, 'and I am glad to see that her sister is with her.' Mrs Bailey turned to us. 'Mrs Roper is a schoolmistress, in fact the head, and therefore very sensible. I will not make any enquiries. I don't wish to intrude.'

Holmes understood the implied warning in her statement. 'And neither do we.' We rose to leave. 'If you see Mrs Smith, kindly let her know I have called,' added Holmes.

As we left, we bowed politely to Aunt Jane, and she raised her head and gave us a crafty look. Her face was shrunken and wrinkled but the skin was pale and soft, like a peach that had dried in the sun. 'People think I don't know what goes on round here, but I do,' she said.

'Oh, take no notice,' said Mrs Bailey to us quietly. 'She has her fancies, you know. They keep her happy, but I don't pay them much attention.'

'That hussy!' muttered Aunt Jane, a sudden glance suggesting that she was referring to someone in Park Villa next door. 'Making great eyes at him, but I know her type. She ought to be ashamed.'

'Hush now,' said Mrs Bailey as she ushered us out, before more embarrassment ensued.

As we walked back to the main road we passed by Park Villa. The door opened and the Smiths' maid came out holding a mourning wreath, which she hung in place under the knocker. A tall, strong-faced young woman, she turned and stared at us accusingly, as if daring us to comment. I could not help wondering if this was the hussy Aunt Jane had mentioned, and if so, who had received her interested glances. We said nothing and walked on.

CHAPTER SIX

'Of course,' said Sergeant Lestrade, 'when we decided to interview all those present at Mr Smith's outburst, the name at the top of most people's lists was Professor Owen, but oddly enough I decided to come to you first.'

'I am flattered,' said Holmes.

We were seated around the table in my rooms in Farringdon, discussing recent events over a pot of tea. Lestrade, stretching out his legs for comfort, had already consumed two pourings of the hot beverage with speed and relish. I thought policing must be thirsty work. The subject of why we had both been at the unveiling of the great auk had already been covered, as had the extent of Holmes's interest in extinct flightless birds, which he declared to be 'non-existent.'

Lestrade told us that the inquest on Charles Witwer Smith, aged thirty-six, had opened the day before, just long enough to confirm the identity of the corpse, and was then immediately closed for further investigation, which, it was strongly implied, might take some considerable time. The bereaved mother had been unable to attend.

'I have sent a message of condolence to Mrs Smith,' said Holmes. 'Is there anything else you can tell me?'

'Right now, we are thinking of robbery as the most likely motive,' said Lestrade. 'A stranger or strangers who simply saw their chance with a well-dressed gentleman, the type who always has a watch and money in his pocketbook and has incautiously wandered into a place out of the public view. But —' and he laid great emphasis on that word — 'we cannot ignore the fact that Mr Smith did succeed in annoying and in some cases deeply offending numerous persons within a very short time after his arrival in London. He wrote a great many letters to Professor Owen, making all sorts of accusations and demands. When that failed to have the desired effect, he managed to obtain a ticket to the unveiling you attended, where he upset all those present, respected men who have given long service to the British Museum, as well as Professor Newton, and Mr and Miss Caldie.' He folded his arms and stared back at us both. 'Would you care to comment?'

'Are you looking amongst them for suspects?' asked Holmes. 'My observation is that when men of science disagree on academic matters, they do not usually resort to murder. They tend to write sharply worded articles for the journals or insult each other in public debate.'

Lestrade was obliged to accept this point and nodded agreement.

'Murders in such circles are most rare,' Holmes continued. 'There was that squalid incident at Harvard Medical College a good many years ago, but in that case the chemistry lecturer did not dispatch a fellow lecturer over a scientific principle, but a man to whom he owed money.'

'Ah, yes, I may have heard talk of that one,' said Lestrade, scratching his head. 'Nasty business. Didn't he burn the body?'

'He did. In the laboratory furnace. And,' added Holmes rather pointedly, 'the murderer would have escaped justice if it had not been for an observant janitor.'

Lestrade drained his teacup for the third time. 'I know what you are saying, Mr Holmes. I can assure you that no one knows better than me how a sharp and vigilant member of the public can be the key to solving a mystery. The police can't be everywhere at once. That being the case, I would be most obliged if you could keep your eyes and ears open for anything that might come your way. In an advisory capacity only, of course.'

'Of course,' said Holmes, with a little smile. 'But if I am to be an advisor to the police, I must ask you to be kind enough to provide me with all the information at your disposal. I appreciate that anything you tell me which has not been released to the public must be treated with the strictest confidence.'

Lestrade gave this some thought, but I could see he was finding a way to acquiesce. 'There are not many members of the public I would do this for, Mr Holmes,' he said at last, 'but you have shown yourself to be worthy of my trust. And Mr Stamford, too. It is always an advantage to have a medical man at your side.'

The 'medical man' sent for another pot of tea and Lestrade launched into his account. Much of what he had learned had been communicated to him by Mrs Roper, since her sister was still too distressed to be interviewed.

Following the unveiling of the great auk, Charles Witwer Smith had been conducted to his home by officers of the museum. He had arrived in a somewhat calmer mood than he had exhibited earlier, although his mother, seeing his agitated manner, had seen fit to ask Dr Scales to call on him. Once assured of his generally excellent health, Smith had had a long and heartfelt discussion with his mother, who had begged him to put all his worries behind him. He promised that for her sake, he would try.

A few days of rest and careful thought had resulted in a fresh appreciation of the right thing to do. Smith recognised that he had been at his happiest in New Zealand and decided that it would be best if he returned there. He then outlined his plan to his mother. He thought that neither of them would find peace or contentment in London, and he did not want to leave her alone in a house with such terrible memories and notoriety. He suggested that they both sail to New Zealand and make a permanent home there. It might take a month or so to make all the arrangements, but he would see about securing their passage and arranging for the letting of the house. His salaried position in New Zealand had been held open for him. Mrs Smith wholeheartedly agreed to the plan.

Smith then wrote his letter to Holmes and went out to post it, telling his mother that he was going to see Mr Selby, his assistant at the *Natural History Review*, which had a one-room office some ten minutes' walk away. There, he asked Selby if he would be willing to assume the editor's chair if it became vacant, and Selby was agreeable. Smith then disclosed his intention to return to New Zealand, the next step being to find a tenant for the house. It so happened that Selby, with a young and growing family, had been looking for larger accommodation within his means, and with the promised increase in salary, he was amenable to renting Park Villa.

Mrs Smith had known nothing of this rapid advancement of her son's plans. When he did not return home for dinner that evening, she went to see Selby, who informed her that Smith had departed after their meeting in good health and spirits, saying he had further business to attend to. Mrs Smith returned home and waited, but when her son had not come home the following morning she went to the neighbours, none of whom had seen him. She then called on Mr Selby again, who had nothing more to add. After that, she went to the newspaper office in case he had gone there, then to the local shops and businesses, and finally to the British Museum. Returning home and finding her son had still not come back, Mrs Smith went to Islington Police Station to report him as missing.

Meanwhile, Charles Smith's body had been found.

'It appears,' said Lestrade, 'that after his meeting with Selby, he went to make enquiries at the New Zealand Shipping Company, which has an office on Bishopsgate Street. It is some two miles or so from the office, and the weather being mild, he might have chosen to walk, or he could have taken a cab. We are looking for witnesses to the walk, and also trying to locate a cab driver who may have some information to offer. The clerk at the shipping company recalled Smith's visit, during which he asked for a list of sailings offering passage to New Zealand. He did not leave his name or address but mentioned that he would be travelling with his mother. After that, it seems that he sought refreshment nearby, in Camomile Street. We are making enquiries at the two taverns there, the Mailcoach and the Saracen's Head, to see if anyone recalls seeing him and who he might have been drinking with. Every public house must have its share of dubious characters, and I suppose the Camomile Street hostelries will have theirs.'

'Was he seen in company with another person at any time that afternoon?' asked Holmes. 'What about when he made enquiries at the shipping office?'

'He was certainly unaccompanied when he left his home and when he saw Mr Selby. He was also on his own when he arrived at the shipping office as far as the clerk can recall. We are still trying to establish the rest of his movements.'

'Where and when was the body found?'

'It was in a shared yard where deliveries were made to the taverns and the nearby coffee house. The body had been hidden under sacking behind some refuse bins, where it was found at first light the next morning. It so chanced that the bins were due to be emptied and when one was moved, the carrier saw a man's hand protruding from under the sacking and raised the alarm. The deceased was not identified immediately as his pocketbook and watch had been taken, but a card was found tucked in an inside pocket, giving a name, "C. W. Smith" and an address in New Zealand. The local police thought at first he might be a visitor staying in a hotel, and made the usual enquiries on that basis, but when they learned that a Mrs Smith had reported her son as missing, she was fetched to look at the body and was able to identify it. It was a highly distressing scene.'

I could sense from Holmes's expression, a quietly reflective look, that he had effortlessly absorbed all this information. 'The cause of death?' he asked.

'I don't think there will be too much difficulty over that,' said Lestrade confidently. 'There was an obvious wound on the back of the head, but also signs of a violent struggle, which may have taken place after he was struck, and it seems that he was finally throttled as he lay on the ground. Two methods of assault: one with a weapon and one without, which suggests that there were two assailants, and we are already interviewing suspects, men with records of violent crime who drink together. There is a great deal of work still to be done, but it is hoped that by the time the inquest re-opens we will have the killers in custody. Even if we can only find one of them, a man of that kind often talks freely to try and incriminate his partner and save himself. Of course, they will both hang. The watch has not appeared. I expect it has been pawned by now and we are making enquiries for it.'

'Were there any clues found on the body which might have come from direct contact with the murderer?' asked Holmes. 'What weapon do you think was used?'

'There were some wood splinters in the head wound, and we will be speaking to two brothers, carpenters who were carrying out some work locally. But there was nothing else of note. A yard which serves three hostelries has a great deal of debris scattered about, and whatever dirt and rubbish was found on the victim's clothing might have simply been from his lying on the ground and have nothing to do with his attackers.'

Holmes looked displeased. 'I wish I might have been permitted to make a judgement on that,' he said. 'And no-one heard anything?'

'No. The noise from the taverns might easily have covered any suspicious sounds. And it is possible that the initial blow partly stunned him, and he did not cry out thereafter.'

'Is there any approximation of the time of death?'

'I am waiting for the police surgeon's full report, but we think he was attacked on the same afternoon, not long after his visit to the shipping company.' Lestrade paused. 'Do you have any observations, Mr Holmes?' he asked, hopefully. 'Anything that might further our enquiries?'

'Not yet,' said Holmes, brusquely, 'but I suggest that the victim's clothing should be sent to Barts for examination by Professor Russell. There may be unexplained residue which will help to positively identify the murderer. The professor will also want to see the final post-mortem report with a description of the injuries.' Holmes did not need to mention that he had assisted Russell before, and clearly anticipated assisting him again.

'I can't promise anything, as the police examiners are still at work,' said Lestrade cautiously, 'but I will see what I can do.'

'When will Mrs Smith be well enough to be interviewed?'

'Her doctor advises against it for the time being. Her sister is looking after her. But when she is well enough, I will let you know, and if you wish to speak to her, I will see if she agrees.

Of course, by then we may have the killers in custody and there will be no need to trouble her.'

Holmes did not comment on that last point, but I could see he was not as confident as the sergeant of a rapid resolution. 'The museum believes that it was Smith who went to the press and divulged what happened at the unveiling of the great auk specimen,' he said. 'This has caused significant professional embarrassment. Have you established whether or not this was the case?'

Lestrade allowed himself a smile. He clearly attached little importance to any discomfort the sensational articles had caused the museum. 'Now you mention it, when Mrs Smith reported her son as missing, she did refer to the newspaper reports. She said he had seen the papers and thought that someone at the museum must have spoken to the press to discredit him and make him appear to be mad. So it looks to me as if each side is blaming the other. Not that we'll ever find out the truth of it now.'

'Had there been any pressmen at the house?'

'I don't know. She didn't mention any. Are you concerned with that?'

'I dislike unsolved mysteries, however trivial,' said Holmes. 'I wouldn't entirely rule out Smith as the man who went to the newspapers, to give publicity to his claims against Owen on behalf of his father. But I think he would have gone to the office or sent them a note rather than invite someone to his home. It was not the story they printed, but that does not mean anything. Whether this has something to do with Smith's murder, I cannot say.'

Lestrade remained unimpressed with that aspect of the tragedy, and having consumed most of the second pot of tea, he left us, promising to ask for the requested materials to be sent to Professor Russell.

The account of Smith's death had reminded me of Dr Woodley's comment that flightless birds were clubbed or throttled by collectors rather than shot, to preserve the skin. 'Holmes,' I said, 'this may mean nothing, but has it occurred to you that Smith might well have been killed by the same method employed to collect a great auk?'

'It tells me that the killer did not have a gun or garotte, or if he did, he did not choose to use them,' said Holmes. 'And now I suggest we go on a little journey without any further delay.'

I had my studies to attend to, as I had a paper to write, but it never occurred to Holmes that I might have demands on my time of greater personal importance than his investigations, and it never occurred to me to refuse him. I anticipated that my next study session would be lit by the proverbial midnight oil. I did not ask where we were bound, as it was obvious that Holmes wished to visit the scene of the murder. What he hoped to find in a place already thoroughly examined by the police I did not know, but I felt sure that if there was anything of importance there, he would find it.

CHAPTER SEVEN

Camomile Street was a busy lane tending east off Bishopsgate, with a dingy array of taverns, coffee houses, narrow shopfronts with apartments above, and tall, looming warehouses. Carriers' carts rattled back and forth, and there was no lack of foot traffic. We entered the yard where Smith had been murdered by passing through an arched entrance large enough to admit delivery wagons, and found ourselves in a cobbled space, open to the elements. Here was all the dust and debris one might expect from crowded hostelries, as well as a stack of discarded broken furniture and a pile of filthy sacks. The pervading smell was of rotting vegetable matter, meat bones, and stale beer.

The refuse bins were ranged against one wall, with very little space available to hide a corpse behind them, but I recalled that Smith had been a slightly built man. I thought it would have been possible to put him there without moving the receptacles, then pile sacking on top. If the bins had not been moved the next day to empty them, a corpse might have lain hidden in such a place for some little while before natural decomposition overcame the prevalent odour sufficiently to draw attention to its presence.

Holmes on the trail of clues was always a sight to see. On entering the yard, he had become the human bloodhound again, treading carefully, examining everything, sniffing the horrid smell.

'What are you looking for?' I asked.

'I am not sure,' he said. 'But if I am permitted to examine the clothing of the deceased, it will be useful to have a sample of what is here for comparison. There may be something on the clothes which relates solely to his killer.' Holmes, even when not pursuing an investigation, was always prepared to acquire specimens for his research and carried about him what he needed to lift and store materials. I was not therefore surprised to see him take a large envelope and a set of forceps from his pocket and begin to collect broken pieces of wood and torn fragments of paper, as well as small lumps of shapeless rubble. There was nothing obvious to tell us exactly where the crime had taken place. The previous day's wet weather and muddy footprints had obliterated any bloodstains. Holmes continued to move about slowly, covering every inch of the ground and stopping every so often to look at the surface and its detritus in more detail. Then, as he circled about and came near to the carriage entrance, he suddenly halted. 'Hallo, what is this?' he exclaimed, picking up what looked like a piece of soiled paper. He held it up for me to see. 'What do you make of this?'

I stared at the unlikely treasure. It was a piece of used wrapping paper.

'Heavy quality paper, white with a pink stripe,' said Holmes, turning it over to examine both sides. 'And I think you will agree that this looks out of place here. As you see, it has been folded in such a way as to enclose a small object, something in the shape of a box. There are indentations along the folds, signs that it might have been secured by a cord or, judging by their width, I think more likely a ribbon. Nothing written on it, unfortunately. It has suffered somewhat from its time on the ground. There is part of a boot print, see? It must have been used to wrap an item of value that had been purchased, possibly even nearby. It might have nothing to do with the body, or it might have been stolen from Smith's pocket by the murderer, who unwrapped it to see what it contained, put it in his pocket, and threw the paper away. If he simply tossed it aside, it has found its way to this spot only after being blown by the wind, which sometimes forms eddies in walled spaces. No marks left by fingers; he may have worn gloves.'

I didn't like to say so, but I thought it might just as well have been blown into the yard from the street.

Holmes continued his searches, using a stick to rake through debris, but stood up with a grunt of annoyance.

'What were you hoping to find?' I asked.

'The ribbon,' he said. 'It should be here — unless… Hmmm. Let us go in and seek refreshment.'

There was a back door leading into the Mailcoach Inn, where a busy bar area was crowded with small tables and rickety chairs. The wooden floor was thick with sodden rushes, and there was an overwhelming smell of tobacco smoke, spilt beer and something cheap and savoury that had been boiling for some time. To my surprise, Holmes decided to take an interest in the young barmaid who brought our drinks, smiling in the most engaging manner, and offering polite appreciation of her hard work. She was not unattractive, but her clothes bore the tainted odour of the tavern, her apron was stained brown, and there were ragged ornaments in her hair. For one awful moment I wondered if Holmes's appreciation of women, something which I had never previously observed, was strictly confined to tavern maids in soiled clothing, but I need not have worried. I soon saw that he had donned a kind of mask, one suited to his enquiries, and this was not his true self. 'I don't suppose you know anywhere nearby where a gentleman might purchase a gift for a lady?' he asked.

'What sort of gift are you looking for, sir?' she replied.

'Oh, something small, delicate. But it must come very prettily wrapped. My young lady is very particular about that. She likes to untie the ribbon, and then take off the paper. She enjoys the excitement of anticipation.'

The barmaid laughed. 'Oh, I know just what you mean. There is a shop very close to here on Bishopsgate where they have all kinds of little trinkets, Lowen and Son — not that any gentleman has ever bought one for me,' she added with a sigh. 'You might ask there. And a bit of ribbon is always welcome.' As she said this, she patted the pocket of her apron.

'If you have some ribbon to show me, it would help me to make my choice,' said Holmes.

'Oh, this is nothing,' she said with a shrug. 'I just picked it up from where someone had dropped it, and one day I will use it to trim a bonnet.' She drew from her pocket a length of narrow pink ribbon, somewhat dirtied. 'It needs to be washed and ironed,' she said.

Holmes reached out a hand and she passed the ribbon to him. He lifted it up for inspection, and we both saw creases that showed it had once been tied in a bow. 'How charming,' he said. 'And you found it, you say? Where was this unexpected bounty?'

'Oh, I don't like to say it, as there was a man found dead there a few days ago. It wasn't on the body or anything, but it wasn't far from where they found him, just by the rubbish bins.' She waited and Holmes obligingly handed it back.

'I think it can be made very pretty again,' he said. 'And if you cannot bring this one to perfection, you might purchase a new piece,' he added, tipping her a few pennies. At that moment another customer shouted, 'Sally!' She blushed, and with an apology, hurried away.

'You certainly have a way with young ladies,' I said.

'I have studied the behaviour in others,' said Holmes, drily, the winning smile vanishing abruptly from his face. 'Young

Sally may find herself interviewed by the police as a witness. If the ribbon was found there, it may well have been thrown aside by the killer. But let us finish our beer and find the trinket shop.'

The jeweller was only a short walk away on the main Bishopsgate thoroughfare. It was apparent as soon as we entered that we had the right shop, as there were sheets of pink striped wrapping paper and a reel of pink ribbon on the counter. 'I wish to look at some suitable gifts for a young lady,' said Holmes to the gentleman assistant. 'A friend of mine, by the name of Smith, said he purchased something here which was well received. Do you have a note of what it was he bought? It was only a small item.'

The assistant smiled. 'We do keep a note of customers' names in case they wish to return something,' he said, 'but I ought to mention that we do have a great many gentlemen come here named Smith who buy gifts for young ladies.'

'It would have been three days ago, in the afternoon,' said Holmes.

'I will look at our record,' said the assistant. He opened a ledger and after a few moments, said, 'Yes, a Mr C. W. Smith purchased a small jewel box. Gilded. Satin finish.'

'Did you sell it to him?'

'Yes, this is my writing. I recall the transaction. The gentleman had an unusual accent. Australian, perhaps.'

'Was he alone? I mean, was he accompanied by a friend whom he consulted about the purchase?'

'No, he was alone. He didn't consult anyone.'

'May I see an item of similar appearance?'

We were shown a fancy jewel box of a size just large enough to hold a few rings or a small chain. I am no great judge of these things, but it looked nice enough. Holmes examined it to find any markings or maker's impressions. 'Has he or anyone else returned the purchase to you?'

'No, why do you ask? Did the lady not like it? I can't imagine that.'

'I felt obliged to ask.' Holmes looked at the price tag. 'Dear me, I regret that it is beyond my pocket at present. But I thank you for your information.'

The assistant tried and failed to look sympathetic. 'We cannot lower the price, I am afraid,' he said. 'But if you wish to make a purchase, we can arrange payment in parts.'

'I will consider it,' said Holmes, and we made our exit before we were shown anything else.

'I wonder who the intended recipient was?' I said. 'It is not the kind of thing one buys for one's mother.'

'There is a lady in the case,' agreed Holmes. 'I will advise Lestrade of my discovery. If it has been pawned, the police might be able to find it. And then we have another engagement,' he added, producing a note from his pocket. 'I have an appointment for tomorrow morning at ten o'clock. Mr and Miss Caldie would like to speak to us, and I can guess the subject.'

CHAPTER EIGHT

Holmes, I learned, had been busy informing himself about the history of the Caldie family and was good enough to enlighten me on the subject on our way to the meeting.

Sir Andrew Caldie had been the laird of a Scottish estate with a substantial, picturesque but tumbledown country house surrounded by rolling pastures. Neither of these appealed to his grandson and granddaughter. They were the offspring of Sir Andrew's only son, Stephen, an enthusiastic horseman, who had suffered a fatal accident at the age of thirty-two, while riding at speed under a low bridge. The widow, whose brief sojourn in Scotland with her husband had created a strong dislike for draughty houses and windswept hills, despite their intrinsically majestic beauty, had made little delay in returning to the city of her birth, London, to raise her children. Her remarriage at the age of forty-five to a minor Italian nobleman had taken everyone by surprise, and she was now residing in Florence.

Once Sir Andrew's bequest had been suitably settled, a complicated business which entailed resolving the minutiae of a long and rambling will, there was an equal division of land and investments between his two grandchildren. Mr Alastair and Miss Emmeline Caldie had entirely different tastes and modes of life. They shared no interests and had their own circles of friends who did not mingle. Understandably, they occupied separate households. Miss Caldie resided in Clerkenwell, where she shared an apartment with a Miss Mercer, a former schoolfellow, who was also a serious and scholarly lady, and acted as both her companion and secretary.

For some years Miss Caldie had made a particular study of history. She was engaged in writing a lengthy volume chronicling female rulers and had produced an impressive series of pamphlets demanding better education for girls. She also hosted meetings of ladies' societies. I had the impression that her home was a highly personal place which she did not wish to be invaded by men.

Her brother was a different species of creature. His apartments in Kensington, which he shared with a long-suffering manservant, were as well-kept as was possible given his habit of hosting social gatherings of a riotous kind attended by persons of both sexes. I say 'persons' since Holmes told me he had been given to understand that the description 'ladies' and 'gentlemen' was inappropriate.

I have said in earlier volumes of these memoirs that Holmes preferred male to female company, but for him, enjoyment of society was either of a contemplative nature, involving armchairs, pipes and debate, or some form of healthy sport. He would have deplored Mr Caldie's idle and potentially scandalous amusements.

Our meeting with the Caldies took place in the brother's sitting room, which, amongst other things, included his grandfather's collection of sporting guns. There were no bird specimens, which I assumed had all been left to the museum, and only one example of taxidermy, the aged and dowdy head of an antlered deer which stared down at us from the wall with an expression of profound disappointment. There were pictures in plenty, mainly of shooting or boxing, but I saw no sign of any cups or trophies, which Caldie would surely have displayed had he ever won any.

We were greeted with cool dignity by Miss Caldie, and a languid nod of acknowledgement from her brother.

My readers will know that in years to come, John Watson with the very best of intentions often entertained the hope that whenever Holmes met an intelligent single young lady in the course of his work, there would arise some spark of mutual interest possibly even leading to a connection. Watson never recorded whether or not the young ladies concerned took a fancy to Holmes, although in my experience it was not beyond possibility. Despite Watson's hopes, he never observed any attraction on Holmes's part which exceeded his appreciation of objects such as works of art. Holmes did of course take a warm interest in the career of Irene Adler, a lady of singular beauty, courage, and resourcefulness. He referred to her as 'the woman' — a warning, perhaps, to Watson that no other woman would ever compare to her in his estimation, and it was therefore futile of his well-meaning friend to attempt any further matchmaking.

As I gazed upon Miss Caldie, I could not help but wonder if she, being unusually learned and possessed of some beauty, might be the kind of woman to interest Holmes. The more I considered this prospect, the worse it seemed. What a dismal household that would have been! They would have resembled not so much a married couple united in affection and hopes for the future, but two elderly professors, sharing accommodation in order to more conveniently pursue their research and conserve their means. I need not have worried; in fact, it took me very little time to dismiss the thought altogether. Holmes showed no special regard for Miss Caldie, and she had none for him. She certainly did not look like a lady who would appreciate the gift of a decorative trinket box.

If Holmes was indifferent to the sister, his dislike of the brother was tangible. Young Mr Caldie did not sit, he lounged and idled, as if a straight back and attentive expression were just too much trouble. Having more time to study Caldie, I could see the first signs of a life of dissipation in his otherwise handsome face. Throughout our interview Holmes directed his questions not specifically to either sibling but to a part of the room that lay somewhere between the two.

'We have called you here in the hopes that you can provide some enlightenment on the accusations made by the late unfortunate Mr Smith implicating our grandfather in some fraud which we believe was a product of his imagination,' said Miss Caldie. 'Had the matter been kept private as requested, we might have left it to expire naturally, but somehow the press have been informed. I assume you have seen the articles?'

'We have,' said Holmes, and I added my confirmation.

'Before we say anything more,' Miss Caldie continued, 'I wish to learn more about you gentlemen. You cannot fail to know something of our antecedents. The Caldies are an old Scottish family, and our mother is descended from a noble line, possibly with some royal blood.' Miss Caldie did not elaborate on the nature of the royal connection, and it therefore seemed advisable not to press her for more detail. Our hostess waited for a reply.

Holmes was rarely forthcoming concerning his ancestry, but on this occasion, he mentioned his descent from a long-established line of country squires, who while not at the very summit of society, were at least worthy and respectable, and spoke of his great-uncle, a highly regarded French artist called Vernet. He also explained his pursuit of a broad education both at college and Barts.

Miss Caldie turned her enquiring eyes towards me. 'I — er —' I began. I was in some difficulty here, as my origins were nowhere near as exalted. My father was a cabinet maker, and any painters amongst my ancestors confined their attentions to walls and woodwork.

'Come, now,' said Miss Caldie, 'I am sure you have nothing to be ashamed of.'

'No, not at all. My family have all been hardworking people. I was once employed at Barts as a surgical dresser and am now studying to be a surgeon.'

'Education is a powerful tool for advancement,' said Miss Caldie, approvingly. She glanced sharply at her brother as if conveying some message on that subject, before continuing. 'Before Mr Smith's unpleasant demise, I had intended to write to him with a polite request that he withdraw his comments, or at least make a statement that he did not hold my grandfather to blame. That vindication will now never happen.'

'This is the thing,' said Caldie. 'You gents were there and saw what happened. And the police sergeant who spoke to us said that you were good friends of the museum.' He turned to his sister. 'How did you put it, Emmie?'

Miss Caldie winced at the contraction of her name. 'We want an independent enquiry into the accusation. The press reports have been careful to stop short of libel, otherwise we would have taken the appropriate action. The police will not involve themselves, as the worst offence would be slander on the part of Mr Smith, who is now deceased. The public would not take our word for it, as we might appear to be biased. And there is no private detective of suitable calibre. I intend, once the truth has been revealed, to write and publish a pamphlet on the subject.'

'You are anticipating that any enquiry would produce an outcome favourable to your family,' said Holmes.

Miss Caldie paused. 'Of course. Knowing my grandfather, of whom we were both very fond, I am certain that he did not intentionally commit a fraud. I would not rule out some kind of innocent error.'

'You may find it advisable to take no action on the matter,' said Holmes. 'Not everyone reads the newspapers or takes such accusations seriously. Yesterday's news is often forgotten when trampled upon by today's. Your campaign might result in the slander receiving more attention than it otherwise might have done.'

'I appreciate what you say,' said Miss Caldie, 'but there is another consideration. When my grandfather's estate was valued, I saw that my inheritance would enable me to realise an ambition which had formerly only been a hope in my mind. I have already taken steps in the matter by forming a charitable foundation, the Caldie Society, whose aim is to promote the higher education of women. There are schools devoted solely to the education of girls, but they teach either domestic skills, with sufficient reading and arithmetic to manage a household, or they impart the secrets of deportment, music, and fashion, in order for their pupils to secure a suitable husband. As a result, the minds of women are insufficiently stimulated and developed. Some schools even believe it is harmful to the female mind and constitution to educate them more fully. I disagree. Have you observed, for example, that gentlemen who deplore the destruction of bird life for sport, put the blame upon ladies for wearing hats with feathers? And these are the same gentlemen who would have ladies left in ignorance of how those feathers are procured. Is it not a curious thing that when ladies lead campaigns against wanton destruction of birds for their feathers, they are the wives of ornithologists, and are therefore properly informed?'

Miss Caldie had grown quite impassioned on the subject, and her cheeks even acquired a little colour. 'But I digress. The point I am making is that I do not want my family name, and the name of my educational foundation, to be sullied with an unfounded accusation of fraud. The Caldie name is very highly regarded. It is the stamp of probity on all matters financial. I and my assistant, Miss Mercer, have been putting all our energies into the Caldie Society and it is due to be officially launched into the world in a month's time, when we will be asking for subscriptions.'

'You wish the matter to be settled in a month?' queried Holmes.

'I hope it can be, or at least something might be uncovered that casts doubts on the accusation, such that any sensible person would dismiss it.' She took a deep breath. 'There is another reason I should mention. Last winter, I was attacked by a serious illness. Alastair —' she nodded at her brother, who made a grimace — 'was also taken ill at the same time. I feared that I was close to death. We are both fully recovered in health, but it impressed upon me the fragility of human life, even to someone as young as we, and I do not know how much time I have to realise my ambitions. Many years, I hope, but we can never know these things. I cannot waste a moment.'

Holmes nodded, then asked, 'Did your grandfather leave any notes on his work?'

'He left a diary and the notes he made in preparation for his book. If you agree to undertake the enquiry, we will provide you with all his papers.'

'You must have read this material yourself?'

'I have, although I have made no special study of ornithology. I have found nothing to suggest anything other than a passion for his collection.'

'You have visited his workshop?'

'Yes, we did so when the estate was being valued.' Miss Caldie wrinkled her nose at the memory. 'I was pleased to leave the actual disposal of the materials to others.'

'Did your grandfather work alone, or did he employ assistants to whom I might speak?'

'His butler, McCaskie, who had a world of patience few may command, was his greatest asset in the work, but he died five years ago.'

'He left no notes or correspondence?'

'All the available papers have been brought together, and I am content to turn them over to you for your examination.'

Miss Caldie did not wait for our agreement; she simply assumed it and beckoned to her brother, who eased himself reluctantly from the comfort of his armchair and fetched two leather cases with stout handles, both of which appeared well stuffed with material. These were deposited in front of us. That was the conclusion of our business, which ended with the formal exchange of cards.

One day Holmes would be able to ask for and receive a tidy fee for his work, but at that juncture it would have been embarrassing to mention payment. After solving the *Gloria Scott* mystery, which he later recounted to Watson, Holmes had formed the ambition of becoming a professional consulting detective, but he was still a long way from achieving this. He had yet to tell anyone, not even close friends or family, of his intentions. Thus, he appeared to be no more than a gentleman dabbler, albeit one to be respected. He was busy acquiring the skills and knowledge of every subject he believed to be necessary, and in addition, forging the connections in those areas of society which might advance him. The Caldies, an old and venerated Scottish family, were eminently suited to join this growing circle.

CHAPTER NINE

Before Holmes could commence his examination of Sir Andrew Caldie's papers, he had another appointment, which he expected me to attend. He was due to see Charles Smith's former assistant Mr Selby, who had been so unexpectedly elevated to the editorship of the *Natural History Review* shortly before the death of his superior. The office of this journal was a single rented room above a hatter's shop in Islington. Mr Selby, who worked alone, greeted us, and we saw at once the creases of distress around his eyes. He was about the same age as Smith, with the kind of neat very short hair that required little grooming apart from a touch of oil. His desk showed he was a tidy sort of man, who liked few distractions and no mess. Apart from something in a silver frame, only the essential implements of his work were to hand. Even the pile of clean notepaper was a perfect rectangle.

The room was simply furnished, the only decorations being framed prints of zoological and botanical subjects. There were no examples of the taxidermist's art. Boxes of recent publications were awaiting distribution, exuding a slight chemical odour of freshly printed paper. Their numbers suggested a relatively small circulation.

Since we were strangers to him, Selby's greeting was perfunctory and cautious. 'How well did you know Smith?' he asked. 'He has never mentioned your name.'

'We had only met him once,' said Holmes, as we were seated. 'We were both present at the unveiling of the great auk exhibit at the British Museum when I found it necessary to pacify him during his outburst. He wrote a very kind letter to me afterwards.'

'I should have gone with him,' said Selby unhappily. 'I knew of his complaints against Professor Owen and feared that he might take the opportunity to confront him. As it transpired, it was even worse than I had imagined. But there was a problem at the printers that day which had to be resolved, and I was obliged to miss the event.' He frowned. 'What, if I might ask, is your interest in this?'

'When Mr Smith was found to be missing, his mother wrote to me asking if I had seen him,' said Holmes. 'I have promised to be of service to her. I am sure she would want to speak to you, but at present she is far too unwell to consider it.'

Selby sighed. 'I attended the inquest on Professor Smith, and now the poor lady has a new horror to face. It's unimaginable. I have sent her a letter of condolence, of course, but I do not expect an early reply.' His expression cleared a little. 'So, gentlemen, how might I help?'

'I have been tasked with making some private enquiries on the subject of Mr Smith's death,' said Holmes. 'It does seem very probable that it was the result of a robbery by a stranger, and that is certainly the theory being pursued by the police, but there has been some speculation that he might have had enemies. Perhaps you could tell me what you know about him. My main concern is I do not wish the police to waste their valuable time on unfounded rumours. Neither do I wish to distress Mrs Smith any further.'

'No, of course not,' murmured Selby. 'Well, I suppose you should know that Smith and I were at Edinburgh University together. The same year and courses, general sciences with zoology and anatomy as our special studies. That was where we first met. After he went to New Zealand, we corresponded regularly. He did valuable work there and supplied many articles for the *Review*. Professor Smith also wrote for us. I joined the *Review* when it was founded eight years ago. In fact, I was offered the editorship when the former editor announced that he would retire, but I was not best placed to take it up then, as I had other more domestic matters to occupy me and could not agree to more time at my desk.' He glanced at the silver frame, and as he did so the signs of strain about his eyes softened and relaxed.

'Your family?' asked Holmes. 'Would you permit me to take a look?'

'Yes, of course,' said Selby.

Holmes turned the frame around and we saw a photographic portrait of Selby standing proudly beside the chair of a cheerful lady with two young children at her side and a baby on her lap. 'How very charming,' said Holmes. 'I can understand your devotion.'

'Yes, well, one has to find a way to account for both expense and time,' said Selby, 'but I believe that the rewards of family life are the greatest happiness a man can have. As it so happened on that occasion, Smith had already told me he was on his way back to London and was looking for a position with a salary. I recommended him, and he was appointed without question.'

'I understand that Smith was acquainted with Professor Newton?'

'Yes, they were introduced recently at an ornithological society. And we had both met Sir Andrew Caldie when we were at Edinburgh.'

'Indeed?' said Holmes. 'The famous collector? What is your memory of him?'

'He gave the students lectures, just informally — he was never employed by the university. He was supposed to be telling us about his collections and methods. But I think he really liked to talk about his adventures as a young man. He had travelled widely, mainly to the Americas, and shot a great many specimens which he preserved for science. But as he grew older, he became somewhat corpulent, and suffered from gout, so he travelled less and purchased what he wanted. Some of the students were active in providing him with specimens.'

'Including yourself and Smith?'

'No, we were not of the shooting fraternity. It can be an expensive pastime, and we were more interested in the natural history of seabirds.'

'I understand that flightless birds are easier to capture,' Holmes observed, his manner deceptively casual. I could see that as he drew nearer to the object of his quest, he was obliged to proceed with great care so as not to break his promise to the museum.

'They are,' said Selby, 'but there are none now anywhere in the Isles of Britain. They do not thrive in populated regions.'

'The British Museum has an older specimen of the great auk collected in the Orkneys,' said Holmes. 'I was able to view it very recently. Do you know if Sir Andrew ever travelled to those regions?'

'Not as far as I am aware.'

'He never mentioned the Orkneys or any other such place in his lectures?'

'I can't recall him doing so.'

'What years were you at Edinburgh?'

'We went up in 1858 and graduated in '61. I stayed on for two years after that.'

Holmes merely nodded, but I could see where his thoughts were tending. If the auk in the museum had been collected for Sir Andrew by an Edinburgh student in 1855, it was before Smith and Selby's time.

'When did Smith develop his interest in flightless birds?'

'I'm not sure exactly, but he became somewhat enamoured of them after attending a lecture, I suppose because they are so extraordinary. After he left Edinburgh, he joined a team going out to New Zealand to study the moa.'

'I can certainly understand why ornithologists find the flightless birds so very fascinating,' said Holmes, warmly. 'Do you have any observations on the specimen of the great auk Sir Andrew bequeathed to the museum? Do you know why Smith took such objection to it? Did he discuss it with you?'

Selby paused for thought. 'He did. He only had a few moments to look at it, of course, but he felt sure that it was not an entire skin. I am wondering if Sir Andrew had purchased something which required repair and added material from another source to make a better display. There is nothing wrong with that, had he made his actions clear, but it appears he did not. It might have been something he kept for his own private appreciation, but his neglect to label it properly or supply details of his reconstruction work enabled the museum to claim it as entire. But it must have been many years ago, and with the passage of time, his memory might have faded. And his executors were not knowledgeable enough to do more than take it at face value.'

'Have you seen it yourself?'

'I am afraid not. I did go, but I found it had been withdrawn.'

'Professor Beare and Dr Woodley have both told me they are satisfied with it,' said Holmes. 'Surely that is proof enough?'

Selby looked doubtful. 'I am not convinced. Beare might have been too eager to approve such a prestigious item, and Woodley is devoted to his mentor and would not have opposed him. At any rate, the important thing to understand is that Smith's anger was not directed at the great auk, or the museum or Sir Andrew, but at Sir Richard Owen. He held Owen to blame for his father's despondency, and thereby his sad death. He had written to Owen many times to demand the proper labelling of the specimens his father had donated so as to give him the credit he deserved, but his letters were ignored. And then he heard that Owen was preparing to publish an extensive study on the flightless birds of New Zealand, with special reference to the moa. Smith feared, and not without reason, that Owen would appropriate some of his work without giving him any credit.'

'You believe that the unveiling was actually an opportunity to confront Owen with his complaints,' said Holmes.

'Yes. I think the great auk specimen was nothing more than the focus of his frustration. A means of attacking Owen's credibility.'

'Smith and Owen had never before met face to face?'

'No. When Smith applied for a ticket to the event in his capacity as editor of the *Review*, he gave his name as Charles Smith, in the hope that Owen would not realise he was the same C. W. Smith who had been writing to him. I am not sure Owen would have personally approved the attendees, but he couldn't take that chance.'

Holmes deliberated for a while. 'Leaving these academic matters aside, do you know of any enemies Smith might have had — I mean persons who would try and do him physical harm?'

'No, not at all. I can scarcely imagine it. I asked the police how he died, but they wouldn't or couldn't tell me. I suppose that will have to wait until the resumed inquest.'

Holmes said nothing.

'Although…'

'Yes?'

Selby wrung his hands in a distracted manner before he spoke again. 'Mr Holmes, I am about to mention something that you might think of no importance. I may be wrong, and I sincerely hope I am, but if I am right and it endangered Smith, then it might also endanger me.' He cast an anguished look at the family portrait.

'I will tell no-one else without your express permission,' said Holmes.

'Thank you. If Smith had any enemies, it can only have been centred around the museum. He hinted to me once that he had a good idea of where that skin came from and when it was collected. He even thought he might know who had collected it. He didn't have the proof, but he hoped he could get it.'

'How did he intend to do so?'

'He wouldn't say. But not long afterwards he told me of a journey he was planning to make. Before he returned to New Zealand.'

'Did he say where?'

'No. But he said that once he had returned with what he was seeking, there was someone he intended to confront.'

'Did he think that person would be unhappy with what he found?'

'Oh yes,' said Selby. 'Very unhappy indeed.'

CHAPTER TEN

Holmes had spent many hours studying the diaries of Sir Andrew Caldie, which extended over three volumes and several years. The task, Holmes complained, was almost an exercise in translation from an obscure text. Not only was the manuscript littered with references which were foreign to him, but the handwriting, of a naturally loose, thready appearance, had degenerated over time into a careless scrawl, omitting letters, and neglecting the dotting of the i and crossing of the t. Sir Andrew himself, Holmes declared in exasperation, would have had some difficulty in reading it.

I thought it would be helpful if I read Sir Andrew's book on preserving birds. Anatomy is a subject which has long fascinated science. It formed an important part of my studies, and it is interesting to see how the organs and skeletons of lower creatures have structures which may be compared to those of men. The wings of birds and the arms and hands of a man are a case in point.

Sir Andrew Caldie's book was not intended to be a scholarly work, but a guide for young naturalists who wished to collect, preserve, and study birds. I found it highly informative about the man, his interests, and methods. In common with many naturalists of his day, and I believe this included both Professor Beare and Dr Woodley, he had initially developed his interest in the subject as a youthful sportsman, when shooting game birds. These birds would later appear suitably prepared and dressed, on a gentleman's table, but young Caldie became fascinated by the mode of life of the feathered creatures, and the miracle of flight.

Nowadays, of course, we have the Royal Society for the Protection of Birds, but in those days, feathers were all the rage in fashion, most birds were regarded as moving targets for sportsmen, and the ornithologist regularly killed the thing he loved in order to study it.

The young naturalist, stated Sir Andrew, must first catch his bird, and he was generous with advice on how this might best be achieved while causing the least possible damage to the specimen, especially the beautiful plumage. He wrote extensively on what guns to select for the purpose, and the importance of using ammunition which would result in the immediate and painless death of his target. If, despite these precautions, a captured bird was found to be still alive, there were gentle means to end its existence with the least amount of suffering. While he preferred the use of the gun, some naturalists had experimented with blowpipes.

The next obstacle was decomposition, and here there was advice on how to delay this until work could begin. One of the best means of preserving a skin was arsenic. The remainder of the book dealt with the finer details of skinning, stuffing and mounting the specimens. Caldie never attempted to elevate his own reputation beyond that of an amateur enthusiast who had devoted many years to his interest, but it was clear that he had considerable expertise in all relevant areas to share.

As I compose these memoirs, I often like to read extracts to my friend George Luckhurst for his comments, but at this point in my narrative I can see he has developed quite a queasy look. He is such a good-hearted fellow, rather fond of animals, and does not like to think of them being harmed. My medical studies must have inured me to the act of anatomising. Sculpture does not offer the same opportunities.

Once our work was complete, Holmes and I met together in a tavern to exchange notes on what we had learned. A pipe for Holmes and a glass of ale for myself assisted concentration, or so we liked to think.

'The diaries of Sir Andrew Caldie, as far as I am able to read them, mainly treat of his travels to the Americas, listing the birds he shot there for his collection, and his later life in Edinburgh,' said Holmes. 'He records visiting the university to give talks to the student ornithological society, to whom he revealed his interest in acquiring specimens in good condition which he would like to purchase. I have found no mention of the great auk, but there is one mention of St Kilda, and as it happens, it was in the year 1855.'

Here Holmes consulted his notebook and read the relevant entry.

'"An interesting acquisition today. I received a visitor who said he had recently returned from seeing his grandmother on the island of St Kilda, and she had given him a specimen, which it appeared had lain neglected in a cupboard for some time. Knowing my interest in collecting birds, he brought to me. It is an *Alca* —" I assume the next letter is a *t* — "rather dry and leathery, very poorly preserved in salt. Parts of it are quite rotten and beyond saving, but I gave him a few pounds, and I will see what I can do with it. It might make an amusing conversation piece."'

'The *Alca*,' I said, recalling what Holmes had told me he had learned during his last visit to the museum. 'That is the razorbill?'

'It is. *Alca torda*, the razorbill, also known as the lesser auk. It is one of the few existing relatives of the great auk, and the only one of the genus *Alca*.'

'You mentioned that it might be mistaken for the great auk if seen from afar.'

'I do not discount that possibility, but on closer inspection, anyone with even slight knowledge of both birds could hardly make such an error.'

'Sir Andrew Caldie must have known the difference.'

'I have no doubt of it.'

'Are razorbills ever seen on St Kilda?'

'They are.'

'And they are not extinct?'

'That is correct. At least, that was the case in 1855.'

I mused upon this for a while. Holmes said nothing, and I sensed that he was merely waiting for me to say something he would inevitably find more amusing than useful. 'Supposing,' I said, cautiously, 'Mr Selby's theory is right, and Sir Andrew, with only a partial skin of this bird, combined it with other specimens in his collection, to produce something that resembled the great auk, just for his own amusement? But if he did so, would that mislead experts like Professor Beare and Dr Woodley?'

'I very much doubt it,' said Holmes. 'The head and beak of the two birds are similar, but the razorbill has wings capable of flight, and the specimen in the museum does not. I am not knowledgeable enough to suggest what other species could have been combined to make such an assembly, even by an expert. But whether this is a whole or partial skin can only be determined beyond doubt by destroying the specimen, something we have promised not to do. Perhaps our optimistic experts inferred that the specimen was a previously unknown subspecies, which would explain the differences in form. But,' he added, with a dismissive gesture, 'all this is mere conjecture. I would like to be much surer of my ground before I make even a suggestion of error to two such distinguished and learned gentleman.'

'We don't know when it was actually collected,' I said. 'Since it had been preserved in salt, it might be quite old, which would dash Professor Beare's hopes.'

'There is only one way we might learn the truth,' said Holmes. 'By going to St Kilda. The population is very small, and if we went there, we would be able to interview them all in a few days. We don't know the name of the man who sold the specimen to Sir Andrew. We don't even know if he was connected with the university in any way, but a grandson who had left the island might be remembered, even if the grandmother herself was no longer alive.'

I waited with some trepidation, as I felt sure that Holmes, who had paused to refill his pipe, was about to suggest a journey to St Kilda. I wondered if I had sufficient warm clothing.

'Unfortunately,' he continued, 'such an expedition is something we have been explicitly warned not to undertake. Indeed, we have promised not to do so. I do not, therefore, intend to attempt it, even in disguise. I will keep my promise until I am released from it. I do not break promises, or they would forever be held worthless.'

'But Smith, as he hinted in his letter, and to Mr Selby, must either have known or suspected the name of the man who sold the specimen to Sir Andrew,' I said. 'Would that be a shameful thing, as Mr Selby suggested?'

'It might, if the man had assisted Sir Andrew in his work, thus collaborating in what is now thought to be a fraud. Perhaps he has a reputation to protect. Professional reputations are highly valued and closely guarded and may be lost over a trifle.'

'Do you have anyone in mind?' I asked, a little nervously, since it had occurred to me that Holmes was alluding to a possible motive for the murder of Smith. As he had said to Lestrade, men do not usually kill for a scientific principle, but I felt sure there must be examples of them doing so to save themselves from ruin.

'I have been studying the yearbooks of Edinburgh University, but no names spring to my attention,' said Holmes. 'We know that both Smith and Selby studied there, but not in 1855. None of the gentlemen we have met at the museum either studied or lectured in Edinburgh. None of them belonged to an Edinburgh ornithological or zoological society. Beare, Woodley and Owen are London men, and Newton is Cambridge. The students at the unveiling are all far too young to be considered, as are the Caldies. Of course, there might be no connection at all with the university.'

'Miss Caldie is determined to protect her grandfather's reputation,' I said. 'But we have seen what steps she is prepared to take. I really doubt she would incite murder. And I cannot imagine the brother stirring himself on behalf of another person.'

Holmes nodded agreement. 'I am missing something, but I don't know what it is. And we are bound by our promise not to go to the very place where I am sure the answer must lie.'

CHAPTER ELEVEN

Holmes, while spending long hours of study and experimentation at Barts, was not undertaking formal courses leading to examinations, and therefore had more freedom in the use of his time than most students. He occupied the next few days in trying and evaluating methods of preserving animal flesh, an activity which only added to his reputation for eccentricity. It was not hard to understand why most of the other students avoided him, or at least regarded him with wary concern. As his closest associate I sometimes found myself attracting adverse comment, but I was already used to that. Having been elevated from my former humble role of surgical dresser, and coming from a family of lower status than those of other students, I was frequently aware that my position in their ranks was questionable.

I was able to provide Holmes with some assistance, but we did not arrive at any conclusions which he found useful, at least not in the case we had in hand.

He was interrupted in the contemplation of his lack of progress by the receipt of a note from Professor Russell, which caused him to smile and exclaim in delight. 'Excellent news! I shall never speak harshly of Sergeant Lestrade again!' He did, of course, on many occasions, but I made sure not to remind him of this vow, said in the heat of the moment and forgotten immediately afterwards. 'The police examiner has agreed to bring the clothing of the late Mr Smith to the chemistry department for further study, together with the full report of the post-mortem. The corpse is not to be ours, but we must be content with what we have. And the professor has accepted my offer of assistance.' Holmes did not actually roll up his sleeves at once, but I think he did so in his mind. 'You might like to attend,' he added, generously. 'Observe carefully and take notes.'

'I would be honoured,' was all I could reasonably say.

The following afternoon I attended the examination and watched Holmes and Professor Russell lay out the clothing of the late Charles Witwer Smith on a bench, arranged in order from head to toe as if it still retained some elements of the body. There was a suit, rather light in weight for the English spring, a shirt and cravat, socks, boots, gloves, and the usual underlinen. The final touch was the placement of a crumpled hat just above the collar.

Holmes had prepared a detailed sketch of the scene of the crime, showing the shape and dimensions of the yard, the positioning of the entrance from the street, and the location of the refuse bins, piles of sacks and broken furniture. 'Part of the area is obscured from the direct view of passers-by, and I believe that is where the crime took place,' he said. 'I have marked with a cross where the body was found, and also where the ribbon and wrapping paper were discovered. They have been examined thoroughly for clues and placed in the hands of the police.'

Professor Russell was studying the report of the post-mortem examination, which included a drawing in outline of the body, marking the location and nature of the injuries. 'The cause of death is given as compression of the neck,' he said. 'But there were other recent injuries, and these together with the clothing should reveal the order of events leading to the fatality. Hmmm. The report also describes bruises found on one wrist and both arms where he must have been grasped tightly. But these are several days old. The altercation in the British Museum, I assume?'

'That must almost certainly be the case,' said Holmes. 'The bruises on the wrist I gave him when I took the hammer from his grip.'

Russell's eyebrows rose a little, but he did not comment. Holmes, tall and of a thin, wiry build, did not appear to be strong, but he was deceptively powerful in action, as those who underestimated him found out to their cost. 'Allow me to demonstrate,' said Holmes. 'Stamford, kindly initiate an attack on me with your pencil.'

One may imagine my fearful anticipation as I raised my arm in pretended aggression, only to have my wrist enclosed in a grip of steel, and my hand bent in such a manner that Holmes easily removed the pencil from my failing grasp. Any further exertion would undoubtedly have caused me severe pain. Professor Russell studied the grip and compared it to the drawing of the post-mortem bruises and declared himself satisfied.

Holmes released my wrist and returned the pencil. 'The arms were undoubtedly bruised when Smith was restrained by the museum orderlies.'

'I concur,' said Russell. 'Moving on to the day of the murder,' he continued. 'First of all, there was a blow to the back of the head. This was undoubtedly the initial assault.' Russell made a careful study of the dented hat, creating a little sketch of his own. 'The damage to the deceased's hat was caused not by a fall to the ground but a blow from a weapon. The report indicates early signs of a contusion and some bleeding, so it was received during life. Holmes, you have an observation on the weapon used?'

'I do. On my visit I saw a great deal of timber and kindling, in particular parts of old furniture that had been broken up for firewood. I took some examples for examination. The shape of the damage to the hat and the contusion described in the report suggest something rounded, like the leg of a table or chair.' Holmes produced a metal tray in which lay a chair leg broken in two. 'I discovered this on the ground in the yard where the pieces had flown after breaking in half. I am fairly confident that this was the actual weapon used. As you see, the blow caused it to break; however, the wood was in poor condition, no doubt the reason the chair was discarded. There are also a few splinters adhering to the collar and back of the coat. I have examined them under a microscope, and they are a good match for this item. Comparing the composition of varnish used would, I think, consolidate that conclusion.'

'We have been told that the blow would have temporarily dazed or stunned the deceased,' said Russell, 'and a blow from an item of this nature would produce that result. The police surgeon is certain that it was not a fatal injury.'

'The deceased was five feet and six inches in height,' said Holmes, reading from the post-mortem report. 'The angle of the injury — and we have been provided with a sketch of the head, which compares well with the damaged hat — suggests that the assailant was slightly taller.'

Russell nodded. 'As a result of the blow, the deceased might well have stumbled and fallen to the ground.' Holmes and Russell moved down the bench, along the layout of the exhibited clothing. 'We can see here that the knees of the trousers are stained with dirt and debris.'

'The toes of the boots and the condition of the gloves clearly indicate that after the fall, Smith was on his hands and knees and making an effort to crawl to safety,' said Holmes. 'One sleeve of his coat has been begrimed with what was probably a kick from the killer's boot, sending him over onto his back.' He lifted the suit jacket for observation. 'His coat is much dirtied on the back. Unfortunately, the mark of the kick on the weave of the material is insufficient to identify the kind of boot, but it should be preserved for comparison should there ever be an arrest. It should also be compared to the partial mark on the wrapping paper. There is a small dark smear which appears to be a common sort of boot polish.'

'The next injury was a broken rib,' said Russell. 'Given the type of fracture, the police surgeon believes that the killer knelt quite heavily on the victim's chest, perhaps even dropping on him. There is, however —' he cast his eyes over the white expanse of shirt — 'nothing on the clothing to show for that contact, apart from some creasing.'

'Had the assailant been wearing working trousers, something might have been left revealing the recent activity, favoured haunts and trade of the killer,' said Holmes. 'But there is nothing of that kind. The garments might have been new or recently cleaned. But the injury as described shows that the killer was heavier than the victim.'

'And finally, the throttling, which it is believed was carried out with gloved hands,' said Russell. 'The bruises are reported as being deep, and the imprints show that the hands were large and strong. Measurements were taken which will assist the police.'

'Are the police looking for two attackers?' I asked.

Holmes and Russell both turned to stare at me.

'They are looking for two men in coarse working clothes,' said Holmes. 'Habitual criminals who often carry cudgels with them. I deduce one man, well-dressed, who did not carry a weapon but picked up one he saw to hand.' He consulted a handwritten document. 'I have here a list of the items found in the pockets of the deceased. I suspect that anything of value has been stolen. A pocket handkerchief, a broken tobacco pipe, and an oilskin pouch with a very small amount of tobacco. The brand name on the pouch was Cameron Brothers. This is an American company which, I have established, also manufactures in Australia, and one must assume distributes its product in New Zealand.'

Holmes glanced at me, as if expecting me to draw a conclusion. I am sorry to say I failed to do so. 'What does a gentleman do whose tobacco pouch is almost depleted?' he asked.

'He — er — buys some more?'

'Indeed. I intend to advise the police that they should make enquiries at the tobacconists along Smith's probable route in case anyone was seen following him.'

As we digested this information and completed the record of the examination, a porter arrived and handed Holmes a note, which he read with interest, but he said nothing until our work in the laboratory was done, and the garments and samples carefully boxed and stored.

'The note was from Lestrade,' he told me as we left to replace the scent of the laboratory with that of a coffee house. 'He tells me that Mrs Smith has sufficiently recovered her equilibrium to permit me to visit, as she is anxious to do all she can to help discover the murderer of her son. I will write to make the appointment.'

'Since the lady is in a frail state of health —' I began.

'Naturally I intend to request that I should be accompanied by a medical advisor.'

CHAPTER TWELVE

I have visited houses of mourning before, even one in which murder had been done, but this one had a character all of its own. All families suffer losses, but some are crueller and more shocking than others. As we approached the door of Park Villa, I struggled to imagine what Mrs Smith must be feeling. She had been the victim of a murderous attack by her husband, who had then cut his own throat before her eyes, and less than three months later, her only son, the best support in her time of grief, had been senselessly killed in a filthy yard. I only hoped that she would have something to tell us which would enable Holmes to bring her the only comfort possible: the arrest of the murderer.

As we approached the house Holmes paused at the corner of the square, glanced at his watch, and looked around. We were a little early for our appointment, and for a moment I assumed he was simply waiting for the hour at which we were expected. I then realised that he had timed our arrival to coincide with the hour at which the death of Professor Smith had taken place. It was a bright morning, the sun well risen, the weather having turned very mild in the last few days. Mrs Bailey's Aunt Jane was sitting on one of the benches in the gardens, a mantle and shawls around her shoulders, and a blanket tucked over her knees. Some young couples were out taking the air and admiring the display of spring flowers. January, when Professor Smith had died, would have been far cooler and darker, with fewer people about. Holmes decided to walk around the back of the little row, where kitchen doors opened onto narrow yards, all of them tidy and well-swept, and with coal holes covered in heavy cast-iron plates. Although the houses were not large, I could see that they were carefully designed to be as easy to maintain and manage as possible.

Following this inspection, Holmes checked his watch once more, and we returned to the square. He gave a nod, seeing on the other side the approach of the coal man's wagon, heaped with sacks and drawn by a large, lumbering horse. The reins were in the capable-looking hands of a young man in the rough clothes suitable for his occupation. Although much begrimed by coal dust, he appeared to be the type of well set up fellow who would turn the head of an impressionable woman. The newspaper portrait had not done his appearance full justice, and an act of heroism will, so I have been told, add greatly to a man's interest.

It was time, and Holmes knocked at the door of Park Villa. The door was opened by the maid, her face framed by a mourning cap, her expression respectful and solemn, suitable for the circumstances. For a moment, however, her eyes brightened as they lingered on the coal man when his cart passed the house. If this was the behaviour to which Mrs Bailey's Aunt Jane had been referring, then the lady had not been imagining the nature of the maid's glances. Whether the situation was harmless or scandalous, I was unable to say. The coal man did not pause, but merely inclined his head in a polite manner. The cart, having reached the far end of the row of villas, made a turn into the back lane for the deliveries.

We were admitted to the house and shown into a heavily curtained parlour where there was very little light from two barely glimmering lamps, as if the two ladies present wished to conceal their emotions in a pall of gloom. Both wore heavy mourning, and everything in the room that might have been bright was draped in black cloth. The maid introduced us and left us there. One of the ladies rose to her feet, offered greetings and asked us to be seated.

'I am Mrs Roper, Mrs Smith's sister,' she explained. 'I am taking care of her and speaking for her when she cannot.' Mrs Roper was about sixty years of age, and being a headmistress, carried herself as such. Although at the time of this meeting I was approaching the age of twenty-three, I suddenly felt myself shrink to the size and age of a schoolboy trembling under the gaze of a particularly critical master.

Mrs Smith was in an armchair surrounded by cushions and shawls. Her hands, enveloped in the folds of a thick woollen muffler, rested on a small black bag.

She glanced up as her sister spoke and nodded, then turned to us and inclined her head in greeting.

We sat down, and as our eyes grew used to the dreadful dullness, we cast our gaze about the room. Facing Mrs Smith was a low table on which there rested two framed photographs shrouded in black ribbon. 'May I take a look?' asked Holmes.

Permission was given, and we looked at the pictures, Mrs Roper describing them to us as we did so. The earliest one was a studio portrait of Charles Witwer Smith taken just before he went to New Zealand. We saw an active-looking slender youth, with only a hint of the whiskers which would adorn his face in later years, facing the camera with confidence. There was also one of Professor and Mrs Smith on the occasion of their being married for twenty-five years. It was apparent that the son resembled the father, since Professor Smith, standing beside his seated wife in a dignified pose, had drawn himself up to appear as tall and wide as possible. Mrs Smith, who had then been in her middle forties, was attractively gowned, her buxom figure accentuated by generous lacing, and undeniably broader than her husband. Since we had recently been gazing at birds rather more than was usual, I could not help but imagine that some people could be compared to birds both in appearance and behaviour. John Watson once likened Holmes to a 'strange, lank bird,' and I certainly sometimes thought of him as resembling a hawk or an eagle. I thought that Professor Smith and his son were like small wading birds, with spindly legs, probing beaks and sharp eyes, whereas Mrs Smith was a plump, rounded hen. I was not sure what bird Mrs Roper resembled, but I would have been nervous to meet one.

'Mrs Smith, I hope this will not give you additional pain,' said Holmes, gently, as he returned the portraits to their place with great care, 'but I have some questions which I hope will assist me in my capacity as advisor to the police to cast some light on this terrible tragedy and bring the culprit or culprits to justice.'

'I will do my best to answer you,' murmured Mrs Smith.

'I was present at the unveiling of the great auk specimen at the British Museum,' Holmes continued, 'and I heard your son's criticism of the exhibit. He later wrote to me saying that there was a person about whom he entertained certain suspicions. He would not name this person until he had obtained proof. I believe he thought that this person was implicated in the situation concerning which he had made those criticisms. Did he say anything to you on the subject?'

Mrs Smith thought carefully, and just as it seemed she might not respond, she shook her head.

'In relation to this subject, did he ever mention Edinburgh University —' here Holmes paused as she required time to think, and again she shook her head — 'Sir Andrew Caldie —' another shake of the head — 'or any other parts of Scotland? The mainland, or even an island?'

At this last, Mrs Smith opened her eyes a little wider. 'Yes, he did mention St Kilda once. He said it was an island, very remote, and an interesting place to study birds, a place he had never had the opportunity to visit. He said — yes, he thought before he returned to New Zealand he would like to go there, if only for a few days.'

'When did he say this? I mean — was it before or after he saw the great auk?'

Mrs Smith sighed. 'It was after, the day after.'

'Did he mention this plan to anyone else?'

'I am sorry, I don't know. He wrote some letters. He —' At this point, Mrs Smith found it hard to continue. She slipped her hands from the confines of the muffler, opened her little bag and withdrew a black-bordered handkerchief, which she pressed to her eyes. There was a carafe of water nearby and deciding to make myself useful, I poured some into a glass and handed it to her. She took it gratefully. As I watched over her, I was able to see some of the scars on her hands from the attack committed by her husband. It must have been a frenzied assault, with great sweeps of the blade, for which she had no protection other than to run and scream, and if cornered, throw up her arms in defence. There were some faint healed scars on her left hand, but the right had been more deeply wounded, with slashes that must have cut almost to the bone. The livid marks with their puckered edges were still clearly visible, and I felt sure that they must have continued to cause her pain. She sipped the water, and once she had had sufficient she handed me the glass, which I placed within her reach. She did not put the handkerchief away but clutched it ready for its next use.

I returned to my chair, and when Mrs Smith looked a little recovered, Holmes continued the questioning in a gentle tone. 'Do you know of anyone who might have wished to harm your son?'

'No, not at all. Why would they?'

'He might have held information which would be detrimental to an individual.'

'He said nothing of that sort to me.'

'Did he ever speak to anyone from the newspapers?'

'No,' she replied in a firmer voice. 'He despised what the newspapers had written, which he said twisted the truth, and he would have nothing to do with them.'

'Did the newspapers try to contact him?'

'Not as far as I know.'

'Did he have any visitors?'

Mrs Smith gave this some thought. 'You mean other than Mr Selby and Dr Scales?'

'Yes, anyone who had not been here before.'

'I only remember one, a man, but he was not from the press, he was from the museum.'

'Did he visit before or after the exhibit was unveiled?'

I could see she was groping for the memory. Mrs Roper was watching her carefully, about to intervene should it prove too taxing for her sister. 'After. It might have been the same day the story was in the newspapers.'

'Did this man give a name? Can you describe him?'

'I didn't see him. He came to the door and was admitted by the maid.'

'I would like to speak to the maid,' said Holmes.

Mrs Roper rang for the maid, who soon appeared and stood before us, her expression so calm as to be impenetrable.

'Jenny,' said Mrs Roper, 'I would like you to tell these gentlemen about the man who came to see my nephew last week.'

'There's not much to say, madam. He didn't give a name. I thought at first he might be a relation of Professor Smith, but he said he was from the museum and wanted to speak to Mr Smith about an exhibit there — a bird. He said Mr Smith would understand his meaning.'

'Did he leave a card?' asked Holmes.

'No, sir, he just said he was from the museum.'

'Describe him. Was he old, in his middle years, or young? How was he dressed?'

'Quite young. Respectable-looking.'

'And Mr Smith agreed to see him?'

'Yes, they met in the study and spoke for some while, then he went away.'

Holmes considered his next words with care. 'I don't suppose you know what they might have talked about? I mean, if there had been raised voices and you chanced to walk past the door at that moment, you might have unintentionally overheard something.'

'I might have,' said the maid, with a little twitch of her mouth revealing that she understood his meaning. 'They talked about something Mr Smith had said which the gentleman wanted him to change his mind about. But Mr Smith said he would never change his mind as he was telling the truth, and he thought he could prove it. I think the gentleman was quite cross about that.'

'One little thing,' said Holmes. 'You said you thought at first that the visitor was a relation of Professor Smith? Why did you think that?'

'He was in mourning,' said the maid. 'At least — he had a black ribbon around his hat.'

The maid had just returned to her duties when we heard a low rumble, like distant thunder, signifying a small avalanche of coal being delivered to the back of the house. At this ominous sound, Mrs Smith suddenly began to tremble, and a sob broke out. I guessed that the noise of the coal delivery, which must have preceded the dreadful events in the breakfast room, had vividly awakened the memory of her husband's death. Mrs Roper went to her sister to comfort her, and then turned to us. 'I am sorry, but I think that is all she can tell you today. I must take her to her bedroom to lie down and give her a draught.'

'Of course,' said Holmes. 'Might we remain, as I would like to speak to you further when you have done so?'

Mrs Roper agreed and conducted her distraught sister from the room.

'The man from the museum must have been Mr Alastair Caldie,' said Holmes. 'He was the only other man present at the unveiling who wore a mourning ribbon.'

'Yes, and he came with the intention of getting Smith to agree to withdraw his accusation,' I added.

'The question to be considered,' said Holmes, 'is what moved him to do so? I am disinclined to believe that Caldie acted out of affection for his grandfather. Neither was it concern about the reputation of the museum, or the science of ornithology, nor any consideration for his sister's charitable enterprises. Mr Caldie thinks only of himself.'

I could only agree.

'Miss Caldie,' Holmes continued, 'has told us that the Caldie name is of some intrinsic value, and I think that it is this which excited her brother's attention. Caldie appears to have no fame or achievements of his own, and whatever reputation he enjoys is that of the family name. There must be more to discover.'

'You don't think he — I mean, he didn't strike me as the kind of individual who could have killed Smith so brutally.'

'You may well be right, but I cannot rule him out of having played some part in it. I will not task him with the fact that he has not revealed the visit to Smith either to me or his sister until I know more. He would only come up with some evasive and unconvincing explanation.'

Mrs Roper returned, and it might have been my imagination, but the room appeared brighter for Mrs Smith's absence.

'Mrs Roper, I cannot express how deeply I feel for your poor sister,' said Holmes. 'She has had two almost unbearable tragedies to endure in such a short space of time. I thought I would take this opportunity to return to her the little hammer which belonged to her son. I thought it best not to hand it to her directly.' He took the hammer from his pocket and handed it to Mrs Roper, who accepted it with thanks and put it carefully away in her pocket.

'I will return it to her when she feels strong enough,' said Mrs Roper. 'And I do appreciate your delicacy and consideration. My poor sister, you see her crushed under the weight of intolerable grief. She is a shadow of what she once was. The slightest thing, a sound, a word, are torture to her.'

'You must forgive me for asking questions of a personal nature, but I wish to obtain a complete picture of her situation in order to progress in my investigation,' said Holmes.

'I will help in any way I can,' said Mrs Roper.

'I understand that the late Professor Smith did not leave his widow comfortably provided for. Or is the neighbourhood gossip incorrect?'

'I don't know what you have been told,' said Mrs Roper, bridling a little at the mention of gossip, 'but it is not far from the truth. The leasehold of this house was of course bequeathed to my nephew, although Phoebe, my sister, was granted the right to live here for the duration of her life, or until she remarries, although there has never been any suggestion that she might wish to. The professor always reassured her that if anything happened to him, she would always have a roof over her head and for that we must be grateful. The books and fossils were bequeathed to my nephew and the household effects and a small annuity to Phoebe. That might have been enough, as she is not extravagant; however, there was a significant drawback we had never anticipated. When the will was proved, we learned that Professor Smith had accumulated substantial debts. He had borrowed money quite recklessly to add to his collection, and the creditors were demanding repayment. Fortunately, when Charles returned he took over the management of all financial matters, and he was able to gain some time by promising to sell the fossil collection, which he hoped would raise enough to pay the creditors, with a sum remaining for Phoebe to invest. In view of this recent terrible tragedy, the matter is now in the hands of a solicitor, and some further time has been allowed. I fear it could take months to settle.'

'Do you know if your nephew made a will?'

'I don't believe so. He was unmarried, although he did have a sweetheart in New Zealand. He told me that when he set sail after hearing of his father's illness, he had been considering sending for her and then marrying and settling down in London, but as you know, he changed his mind and decided to return to New Zealand with Phoebe.'

'Your care of her does you credit,' said Holmes. 'It must have been a terrible ordeal for her to return to this house after the death of her husband.'

'It was, poor thing, but it is her home, and she did not return at once, of course. The police had the run of it for a while, and I took her to stay with me. I had the front window made safe for the time being and sent Jenny back to her mother until Phoebe felt able to come back and say how she wanted things done. The house was in a terrible state. It was weeks later and very cold. The kitchen range had to be properly raked out and there was almost no newspaper to light the fires.'

'The window of the breakfast room has still not been repaired,' observed Holmes. 'Why is that? I am surprised that your nephew did not arrange it.'

'No, well, that has been a difficulty. The room has been locked up. No one goes in there.'

'Not even to clean?'

'Not even for that. Phoebe won't hear of it.'

'Why do you think your sister did not want the room scoured?' asked Holmes.

It was some moments before Mrs Roper could speak. 'I think … I do believe most strongly that her husband's death was such a terrible thing for her to witness that she has closed up the room because if it is locked and never touched, she can somehow imagine that it does not exist. The room and its memories are shut away where they can't harm her. I said she should get Jenny to go in and clean it, but she would not, although Jenny was determined to do so because she said it would smell bad if it was left. I think Charles was trying to persuade my sister to have it done, and the window repaired before they left for New Zealand. But now, poor Phoebe hardly knows what to do for the best, and it is not a subject I wish to raise with her.'

'We saw the coal man making his rounds as we arrived,' said Holmes. 'That must have been her rescuer, Mr Hepden.'

'Oh yes, he still comes the same way.'

'And at the same time?'

'Yes.' Mrs Roper hesitated.' I shouldn't say it, but…'

Holmes raised an expectant eyebrow.

'He seems like a good enough sort, but he has been sweet-talking the maid. I told Phoebe she ought to put a stop to it, but she won't. I suppose she is grateful to him for saving her, and as far as I know it is just talk, but all the same…' She shook her head sorrowfully. 'Is that everything you wish to know, Mr Holmes?'

'Not quite. I would like your permission to examine the breakfast room.'

CHAPTER THIRTEEN

Mrs Roper was both astonished and troubled by Holmes's unexpected request. 'I am not sure about that,' she said. 'Phoebe has very determinedly ordered that the room should not be opened.'

'But both you and your sister have also said you wish to do everything you can to assist my enquiries,' Holmes pointed out gently.

'The enquiries into her son's death, of course. But I really can't imagine how seeing the room where her husband died might help you.'

'I cannot promise it will,' said Holmes, 'but two such tragedies in one family in such a short space of time raise questions which must be answered. Before I continue, I would like at least to reassure myself that the fate of Professor Smith had nothing at all to do with the murder of his son.'

Mrs Roper considered this and as she did so, her hand strayed to a capacious pocket, and her fingertips rested on something within.

'You have the key?' asked Holmes.

'Yes,' she admitted.

'Who else has one?'

'Only Phoebe. She has it locked away. She let me have this one only in case of an emergency, but I have promised not to use it unless it is strictly necessary. Should there be a fire or some other disaster.'

'I would suggest that the murder of her son releases you from that promise,' said Holmes. 'If you allow us to enter, we will do no more than observe. We will touch nothing. And we would be grateful if you would come with us as a guide, to elaborate on what we see and answer any questions.'

Mrs Roper required only a brief consideration, then she made a decisive movement of her head. 'Do you know, I think it is about time it was looked at.' She rose to her feet. 'Come with me.'

Holmes picked up one of the lamps. 'May I?' he asked.

'Yes, I expect you'll need it.'

He turned up the flame, and we followed Mrs Roper out of the melancholy room and down the hall to the door of the room where the tragedy had taken place.

It took only a moment for her to gather herself for the ordeal, then she produced the key, turned it in the lock, and pushed the door open. It made almost no sound.

'And you can assure me that no-one has been in this room since the police left it after the death of Professor Smith?' asked Holmes.

'I can,' said Mrs Roper.

Holmes handed me the lamp, took his magnifying glass from his pocket, and studied the hinges of the door before we went in. The room should have been brighter, given the weather and the time of day, but the boarded window allowed in very little daylight, and we were grateful for the lamp.

None of the rooms in the little villas were especially large, but the breakfast room was a model of domestic peace and intimacy. There was a handsome fireplace bordered by decorative tiles, a set of brass fire-irons, a folding screen, a mantelshelf for family treasures, a round table where husband and wife could enjoy quiet meals and conversation, two comfortable dining chairs, and just enough room for a maid to move around to bring what was required on a tray. At least, that was what this room ought to have been and had once been. It was now a field of battle, from which only the dead man was missing.

The first thing that we noticed was the smell. It was not just that of old dried blood with its musty odour of advanced decay, faintly metallic and almost a little sweet, but there was also the evidence of the barely started meal. The table revealed a breakfast of toasted bread, boiled eggs, and tea, and there were the curled green remnants of what must once have been slices of ham, and dark yellow stains of three-month-old milk. Mrs Roper indicated with a gesture that I could rest the lamp on a little dresser where there was chinaware, glass and drawers for cutlery and linen. She was clearly unused to the smell of decomposition and pressed a handkerchief to her nose.

'Can you tell me where Professor Smith usually sat?' asked Holmes.

'He always sat with his back to the window for the daylight so he could read his journals or a newspaper,' said Mrs Roper. 'My sister did not read at the table, and so she sat opposite.'

As far as I could see, nothing had been cleaned or tidied since the tragedy. Just inside the window there were large pieces of glass lying on the carpet, where the coal man, Samuel Hepden, had broken in.

Holmes surveyed the table, the uneaten food, the soiled dishes and cutlery, the cups with brown crusts of dried tea, the overturned dishes and dirtied tablecloth, a crumpled napkin, and a journal, open at an article on fossils, the pages torn. He did not touch the journal but made a careful note of the name and issue number. Beside the table, a cup and a plate were lying on the floor, their contents spilt. The chair where Mrs Smith had sat was pushed back from the table, but her husband's chair lay overturned on the floor. A little way beyond it was a large patch of blood on the carpet, dried to darkened flakes.

Holmes stared thoughtfully at the stain, then bent down and examined it and its surroundings through his glass. 'This is clearly where the man fell and bled profusely onto the carpet from his throat wound, but I also see many droplets, old stains, which are so darkened they are hard to identify without closer examination.'

'Tea, perhaps?' suggested Mrs Roper. 'If he was agitated, he might have spilled some.'

I could see a clenching movement of Holmes's fingers, a sure sign that he was frustrated. Had things been different, I think he would have cut out that part of the carpet with a knife and removed it to Barts to be examined. Instead, he took his notebook and pencil from his pocket and made a sketch, jotting some observations.

'I also see footmarks,' he continued, 'some undoubtedly left by police boots, and possibly also Dr Scales, who would have had to forgo the usual nicety of wiping his feet as he entered the house. These larger, darker ones leave traces of coal dust, and must be those of Mr Hepden. In fact, if I look closely, I can see where he laid the coal sack against the window to protect himself before he broke it and entered. But the intrusion of half the London police since then has rendered any further examination inconclusive.'

Holmes moved carefully around the table. 'Mrs Smith said that when her husband attacked her, she left the table and cowered beside the fireplace. One might ask why she did not run from the room, but a probable explanation is that her husband had placed himself between her and the door, so there was no escape.' He stood before the fireplace. 'The fire screen has been cast aside and the fire irons have been knocked over. Did she go to them for a means of defending herself? Did she stumble into them, or did he kick them away from her? We may never know. But it was here that he made his attack.' Holmes pointed up the wall; there were dark blotches on the wallpaper. 'And we can see long trails of blood drops spattered up the walls, flung from the razor blade as it cut. There is also blood on the carpet where it fell from her wounds, both large splashes and smaller drops.' Once again, Holmes made an annotated sketch in his notebook.

He turned to face Mrs Roper. 'I have promised to touch nothing, and I will keep my promise. I would be grateful, therefore, if you could open the drawers of the dresser so I may examine the contents.'

'What is it you wish to see?' she asked.

'Merely what is usually kept in this room. You say nothing has been removed?'

'Nothing.'

'Very good.'

Mrs Roper opened the drawers one by one, and they revealed the expected contents. Holmes, staying faithful to his vow, asked her to count what was there, and watched as she did so. Since the table had been set for two and such things often came in sets of six, it was no surprise to find four each of the usual items of breakfast cutlery, and four napkins.

Holmes thanked Mrs Roper and we left the room, which was re-locked. Our hostess, out of politeness, offered to order tea, but not with any great enthusiasm or appetite. We declined the offer and made no request to stay any longer.

'You will let me know if anything is discovered?' said Mrs Roper, hopefully.

'I will. Is it your sister's intention to remain here?'

'I have suggested that she comes to live with me and rents out the house. But it will be a while before she can decide. We must settle the financial matters first.'

We bid Mrs Roper goodbye, expressing sincere wishes for the health of her sister, and she showed us to the door. There were still people about, and we saw the maid of Walnut Villa in the gardens, preparing to assist Aunt Jane indoors. As Holmes and I walked back to Barts in the bright spring weather, a fresh breeze clearing the curious array of odours from our nostrils, I asked him why he had wanted to see the site of Professor Smith's death.

'I thought it would be educational,' he said.

'And was it?'

'Extremely.'

CHAPTER FOURTEEN

The resumed inquest on Charles Witwer Smith added little to our information. Mrs Smith was there, moving very slowly and tremulously, but ably supported and comforted by her sister. They were accompanied by a well-groomed gentleman of about fifty, with a calmly assured bearing and carrying a small medical bag. I guessed that this was Dr Scales. Whether he was there to give evidence, console Mrs Smith, or deal with a possible emergency was unclear.

I hoped that Mrs Smith, who was helped into a chair, would not be called to give evidence, as I foresaw some difficulty in lifting her out of it. She was heavily veiled, as widows so often are, but every so often a mittened hand clutching a mourning handkerchief crept like a crab under her veil and after some unseen motion, was withdrawn again.

Fortunately, the jury had nothing to debate, since they were formally directed by the coroner to return a verdict of murder by a person or persons unknown. The inquest was closed, and all remaining questions were left open, to rest with the police.

Before we departed, we paid our respects to Mrs Smith and her sister, and Mrs Roper was good enough to introduce us to Dr Scales. 'This is Mr Holmes of Barts Hospital and his assistant, Mr Stamford, and they have been advising the police,' she said.

Mrs Smith laid a hand lightly on the doctor's wrist. 'Dr Scales,' she entreated, 'I would be so obliged if you could let these gentlemen know any observations you might have which would help their work. I give you permission to share the confidences of the consulting room, and all your papers relating to my poor family. I know the police have talked to you, but one of their men did speak very highly of Mr Holmes and his methods, and I would not want anything held back from him.'

Dr Scales was blessed with a solicitous tone to soothe the most anxious of patients. He readily bowed his head in assent. 'I will gladly do whatever I can to ensure that the villain or villains who did this are quickly secured,' he said.

'In that case,' said Holmes, 'might I make an appointment to speak with you on the subject? I will also share what I know.'

The arrangement was made for the following afternoon.

'What do you hope to learn?' I asked Holmes later.

'Dr Scales was called to the house after Smith was brought home by the museum orderlies and had a private consultation,' said Holmes. 'He may well be in possession of facts that he does not realise are essential to the case.'

Dr Scales lived on the opposite side of the garden square from the row of villas where the Smiths had made their home. It was a handsome three-storey house, the ground floor of which had been converted to consulting rooms and a dispensary. It was very much a family concern. The brass plate outside the door showed that the practice also included a Mr Scales Jr, surgeon. The dispensary, which we spied through a glass aperture, was in the charge of a neat young lady whose features resembled the doctor's sufficiently that one could be in no doubt that she was his daughter.

An elderly servant conducted us to a warm and comfortable consultation room, where there was a space set aside for the ease of fragile patients who required pleasanter seating than the usual stiff-backed chairs. Here we greeted Dr Scales, who was prepared for the interview with a folder of notes lying on the desk before him.

Holmes began by engaging the doctor's full confidence, saying that he had met Charles Smith at the British Museum, describing Smith's state of agitation, and his subsequent more judicious correspondence. Holmes added for good measure that he had been assisting Professor Russell of Barts in examining the evidence relating to the murder. In the days before his great fame, it was often necessary for Holmes to seek and obtain the trust of professional men before questioning them. In later years his mere name was usually sufficient.

The doctor's initially cautious manner eased, and he became open with us. 'The last time I saw Mr Smith was on the day of his return from the museum after the great auk incident,' he said. 'Of course, I read about it in the newspapers afterwards, but on that day, Smith talked freely of what had happened, and he did mention a young man to whom he was extremely grateful, as that gentleman saved him from a far worse situation.'

It was clear from the doctor's expression that he had guessed that Holmes was that man. Holmes merely inclined his head with a smile.

'His mother had sent the maid with a note asking me to call, as she was worried about her son's nervous state,' Scales continued. 'By the time I arrived, he was moderately composed. He said he had tried without success to put his grievances before the museum, and he now intended to put them before the public. These were grievances against Professor Owen, whom he was sure had caused his unfortunate father's derangement and death. But he did realise it would now be wise for him to spend a little time reflecting on how best to achieve his object. His present intention was to write to the museum directors and also compose a carefully worded letter to the *Times*.'

'He did not consider making a direct and more immediate approach to any newspaper?' asked Holmes.

'No, he wanted to ensure that his arguments were printed in his own words. Clearly that did not happen, but where the newspapers obtained their information, I do not know. I am sure it was not from Smith. It was certainly not from me or Mrs Smith. I do not think,' he added with a smile, 'that those publications can have pleased the museum. But on that day, I duly examined Smith at the request of his mother and found nothing wrong with him, apart from his recent upset. I prescribed a simple calming draught and nerve tonic. There was, however, another matter on his mind, which he confided to me.' There was a short pause before he continued. 'Did you ever meet his father, Professor Smith?'

'No,' said Holmes.

'Smith and his father were very alike, both in appearance and character. Under the circumstances, the son was concerned that he might have inherited the father's instability. They were both, in my estimation, men who harboured deep emotions which they often concealed behind a mask of calm, but that did not amount to anything further. It was a matter of character rather than disease. Smith, however, was afraid that there was a risk he might one day commit the same horror as his father. He was considering marriage and wanted to be sure of his fitness as a husband, and of course as a father. I was able to reassure him that I saw no signs of anything that should dissuade him from marriage and fatherhood. His father had consulted me a number of times, as he suffered from occasional fits of giddiness, but Smith said that he was not prone to them.'

Scales took a deep breath and opened his folder. He spent a few moments consulting the papers before he continued. 'When I returned home after seeing Smith, I looked at my notes recording his father's consultations and treatment. I began to wonder if the professor's fits were an early sign of something more serious, something which if he had lived longer would have become more apparent. The professor did express to me his unhappiness regarding professional matters, but I put that down to the natural rivalries so common in academic life. He also said he had concerns over the behaviour of his wife, which he would not elaborate upon. Again, at the time, I did not give those comments any great weight. In the last week I have consulted my books and spoken to some medical friends.'

We waited patiently while Scales wrestled with his conscience. 'I have yet to express my thoughts to Mrs Smith, as I wish to gather further expert opinions before I do so. I may in time be able to speak to her in words which will bring her some small comfort. But if you will agree to keep my confidence for the time being, I will share with you where my thoughts have been tending.'

Naturally we agreed.

'I think that Professor Smith might have suffered from a tumour in the brain. There are many examples of this in the medical literature and they are quite obvious at post-mortem examination, but since the cause of Professor Smith's death was all too obvious, it seems that his brain was not examined. Pressure of such a growth can result in headaches, which Professor Smith did not suffer from, although he might have done had he lived longer, and sometimes, depending on the position of the tumour, visions, giddiness, and delusions. Men have been known to become convinced that they have enemies plotting their downfall, that their wives are betraying them, all these fears without foundation, entirely produced by their disease, and which have been known to lead to violence and even murder.'

'Is it your theory that Professor Smith's belief that his professional standing was harmed by Professor Owen was merely a product of his imagination?' asked Holmes.

'I took the liberty of speaking to some of his colleagues, who told me that while Professor Owen was considered the pre-eminent man in his field, and with good reason, the decline in numbers of students attending Professor Smith's lectures were mainly due to failures in his memory, which had become somewhat unreliable of late. I was hoping to be able to inform Mr Smith that his father's outburst and death could not be laid at the door of Professor Owen. My intention was to calm his antagonism and set his mind at rest, so he would no longer find it necessary to take any further action. I would also have reassured him that his father's condition, if I was correct about it, was not heritable.'

'Dr Scales, you were the first person to arrive at the house following the death of Professor Smith, after the alarm was raised,' said Holmes. 'I was recently permitted by Mrs Roper to examine the room, which has been locked up unused since the incident. I would appreciate any observations you might have. Please try to recall as much detail as possible.'

'Ah, yes,' said Scales regretfully, 'that was a scene the like of which I never want to see again. When I arrived at the house, there were ladies and servants in the street, all in a great state, and the front window had been broken in. I saw a coal sack lying over the ledge.'

'I understand that the maid was not in the house at the time. Did you see her?'

'No, I believe she had been sent on an errand. I had to climb through the window. It was the coal man who had broken it, and he was able to help me through safely. The maid came back later.'

'The coal man might have gone and opened the door for you.'

'He might have, but I suppose it is a natural thing for coal men not to dirty a house with their working clothes. And I suspect he did not want to leave Mrs Smith alone in that room even for a moment as she was so distressed.'

'That is understandable,' agreed Holmes. 'And did he leave by the window?'

'Yes, I believe he did.'

'I would be most interested to know what you observed when you first entered the breakfast room.'

Scales nodded. Unpleasant as the sight must have been, he showed a wholly professional manner as he made the effort to recall it. When he began to speak it was as if he was there once more, gazing about the death room. 'It was a scene of great confusion. I had to avoid treading on broken glass as I entered. The table had been laid for breakfast, in fact I think breakfast had been proceeding, but the cups and plates had been upset and some of them were on the floor and the contents spilt. One of the chairs was overturned. There was a journal of some sort on the table, but it had been torn apart very violently. I found Professor Smith lying on the floor beside the table, with blood spreading under his body. There was a bloodstained razor on the carpet beside him. I didn't touch it, of course. I saw at once that his throat was cut, and nothing could be done for him. Mrs Smith was cowering near the fireplace, in a state of great distress. Her hands were cut and bleeding. There was blood on the carpet and splashed up the walls. The coal man said that when he broke in, he had found Smith attacking his wife. He had seized the professor to prevent worse injury, and then the man had used the razor on himself.'

'Did the coal man attack or injure Smith? Was he cut with the razor?'

'The coal man was uninjured. I had the impression —' here Scales made a movement with his hands to restore the memory — 'yes, I think he must have come up behind the professor, taken him by the collar or shoulders or arms, and flung him aside. Like a sack of coals, I suppose.'

'And the coal man was not cut by the window glass?'

'No.'

'Did he carry any tools, such as a hammer?'

'He had something on his belt — an iron hook. I think coal men use them to haul sacks about.'

'Had Smith been struck with the hook?'

'No. But the coal man is a strong young fellow, and whether or not he was armed the professor was no match for him. I think when Smith saw his wife was being protected, he must have realised it was all up for him and used the razor on himself. My first duty was to stop the bleeding on Mrs Smith's injuries, which I did with heavy bandages, but I could see they needed more careful treatment. Later I took her to my surgery and saw that the cuts were stitched.'

'When did the police arrive at the house?'

'Not long after I did. I went and opened the front door for them.'

'And when did the maid return?'

'I think it was a few minutes after the police came. I didn't see her, but I heard a constable say she had returned from her errand. She must have come through the kitchen door. They made sure she didn't enter the breakfast room and sent her to her room. I assume they questioned her.'

'Did you examine Professor Smith's injuries?'

'I saw the cut very clearly when the body was being removed.'

'A single cut? Or several?'

'Just one, and a very determined one.' Dr Scales indicated the extent of the wound on his own throat, placing his fingertips just beneath his earlobes. 'His windpipe was cut through, arteries severed. He was dead before I arrived. I made a sketch of it to show the coroner.' Dr Scales extracted a document from his folder, which he showed to us. It depicted a gaping slash across the throat, deeper over the windpipe, narrower at the slightly turned up ends, like a second mouth. 'A suicide will often hesitate before making the fatal cut, and there will be small preparatory marks, but there were none in this case. The poor fellow must have been greatly afflicted in his mind.'

'He was right-handed?'

'Yes. I have no doubt that the wound was inflicted with the right hand.'

As we left Dr Scales, I could see that Holmes was reflecting on what he had learned. I did not see him again for three days.

CHAPTER FIFTEEN

The world should feel grateful that Sherlock Holmes never decided on a career as a university lecturer. It is an oft repeated truism that those whose knowledge is deep and abundant do not always have the knack of conveying it to others less advanced in their education. Holmes shared this fault, and in addition he had a mischievous streak, which meant that he was often deliberately obscure, as if he enjoyed seeing his listeners squirming in their efforts to understand him. When they failed to follow his reasoning, he was derisive in his criticism, and when he finally deigned to explain his conclusions, it was with a witheringly condescending tone. This attitude, which he has maintained throughout his life, did not earn him many friends, although those few who were willing to endure his sometimes lacerating tongue were rewarded with an insight into one of the finest human minds that ever existed.

When he was engaged in a mystery, he often withdrew into his own thoughts as he assembled the information in his possession, and sometimes, as on this occasion, he disappeared altogether without telling anyone where he was going or how long he might be absent.

Since our interview with Mrs Smith, I had been thinking about Mr Caldie's visit to Charles Smith, and both the subject and tenor of their conversation. I agreed with Holmes's interpretation that the preservation of the Caldie name must have some significance in the life of Sir Andrew's grandson, or he would never have stirred himself to make the visit. The opportunity for a little sleuthing of my own had just arisen.

As I have previously recorded in these memoirs, I was no great athlete like Holmes, but I enjoyed an afternoon of cricket in the summer and some light sparring in the winter months. When attending classes at the King Henry rooms, I had met a number of young boxers, one of whom, a useful lightweight called Brandon Molloy, was due to engage in a bout under strict Queensberry Rules at the Wheatsheaf Tavern, one of the more prestigious venues in Kensington. Molloy told me that Caldie was regularly seen there, watching the contests, gambling on the outcome, drinking more than was good for him, and being generally free with his money. It seemed possible that young Caldie might be there on the night of Molloy's bout. Even if he was not, I might be able to learn something about him that would explain his reasons for addressing Charles Smith.

I told Molloy I would go to watch him box, and he advised me that I had best not get involved in any wagers unless I had deep pockets, as the landlord, Mr Gough, who ran all the betting did not like defaulters on his books. I had medium-sized pockets, but they were rarely full, with very little to spare for entertainment.

The Wheatsheaf was one of those sprawling establishments dating from the days of coaching, with capacious accommodation and generous stabling. There was a large green at the back where pugilists could exercise unobserved. I felt sure that illegal bare-knuckle bouts had once taken place there, before development of the area had brought better roads and railways, more dwellings, and greater risks of being invaded by the police. The Wheatsheaf had been obliged to become respectable, or at least appear so.

The tavern, from outside inspection, looked to be to be well-lit, clean, and welcoming. On entering I was able to purchase a ticket for the evening's entertainment; however, having done so, I was immediately approached by a stranger. I shall never forget my first impression of Mr French, a gentleman of towering height, heavily oiled black hair, craggy features, deep-set steel-grey eyes and a determined expression. 'If you don't mind, sir,' he said in an unexpectedly soft voice, 'Mr Gough would like a word.' I was not in any position to object, and was conducted to a small office, where the landlord greeted me warmly.

Mr Gough was, in contrast to his associate, all hospitable smiles. He was a comfortable-looking gentleman of impressive girth, encased in sportsman-like tweed, and smelling powerfully of cigars. 'Mr Stamford,' he said, and I was wondering how he knew my name, when he added, 'I understand you are a student of the art of sparring at the King Henry Tavern in Covent Garden. Molloy has vouched for you, and I thought I would like to welcome you personally to the Wheatsheaf.'

'That is very kind of you, sir,' I said. I thought of adding some compliment about the premises to my statement, but it was one of those situations where I sensed that the less I said the better.

'Now, we like to run a very efficient house here,' Gough went on. 'My associate Mr French —' he nodded in the direction of his tall companion, whose expression remained largely impassive with the merest hint of menace — 'will be happy to advise you if you require any more information. You only have to ask.' Mr French said nothing but glowered at me. I decided I did not need any more information.

'You will be pleased to know that some of our members are very highly placed in society,' Mr Gough continued. 'Very highly indeed. I will say no more, except it would not do to offend anyone.'

I think I stammered out my agreement to his requirements, and he acknowledged my reply with a chuckle of contentment and an open-handed gesture. 'Now, feel free to enjoy your evening, Mr Stamford,' he said.

I was conducted away by Mr French, who showed me to the door which led to the upstairs boxing parlour. I was pleased to see him remain behind when I mounted the stairs, although I could almost feel his glare spearing my back as I went.

The bouts were to take place in a large square room with its own private bar, manned by burly bartenders. They looked like the sort of men who would stand no nonsense but would be able to deal with it efficiently should it arise. There was already a noisy crowd gathering around a roped ring which stood on a platform in the centre, and a sea of top hats was partially obscured by cigar smoke. I looked around and saw young Caldie there, leaning on the bar with a drink in one hand and a cigar in the other. He was surrounded by a group of young men who appeared to be of similar age and enthusiasms. I thought it best to remain unobtrusively in the crowd.

There were several bouts that evening, the first of which was Molloy's, who acquitted himself well against a more experienced man and won by a narrow margin. I cheered him on, perhaps rather too enthusiastically, and he grinned appreciation in my direction.

'Stamford, I thought that was you,' said Caldie, suddenly, coming up behind me and clapping me hard on one shoulder. 'What are you doing, lurking here?' He had clearly been drinking steadily during the contest, and his face was flushed bright pink and shiny with sweat.

'I came to see Molloy fight,' I said. 'We train at the same club in Covent Garden.'

'Do you now? I hadn't seen you as a fighting man. Well, there is a lot here to take your fancy. There's a room upstairs with other entertainments, if you know what I mean. And the gymnasium is second to none. You can have a Turkish massage if you like that sort of thing. I expect you've been introduced to Mr French.'

'I — yes.'

'He'll show you around if you ask him. Ask nicely and pay him well.'

'I'll remember that, thank you.'

'Let's have another drink,' he exclaimed, clapping me on the shoulder again.

I had had no drinks so far, but Caldie was insistent and was steering me towards the bar and his group of friends, when Mr French appeared. For a large man he moved silently and managed to creep up when one least expected him.

I was somewhat relieved when Mr French ignored me, and leaning towards my companion, muttered, 'Mr Caldie, come this way. Mr Gough wants a word.'

Caldie made a brief pantomime of appearing comically frightened, probably to impress me.

Mr French saw no humour in the situation. 'Now,' he said.

Caldie gave a nervous laugh, but did as he was told, and Mr French conducted him away. After a moment or two, I decided to follow. They proceeded down the stairs and through the main bar to the door of Mr Gough's office and disappeared inside. I toyed with the idea of listening in on the conversation but realised that my skills as an amateur sleuth did not go so far as to render me invisible. I headed to the bar and ordered a very small drink, which came at a larger price than I liked to pay. I sat within sight of the office door, placed my drink on the table before me, and resolved to make it last well.

At length the door opened and Caldie emerged. I had never seen a man change so rapidly. He was actually grey in the face, and horribly sober. For a moment I thought he was about to be very ill. He almost fell against the wall and leaned there, taking deep breaths. I went to him, taking my drink with me, and he saw me and uttered some oaths and highly critical expressions regarding Mr Gough, which I will not record. Seeing the glass in my hand, he seized it from me without asking, and drank the contents in one gulp. 'That Smith and his mad allegations!' he exclaimed. 'If he wasn't already dead, I would kill him ten times over! He has hurt the Caldie name beyond repair.' He belched noisily and leaned towards me, grasping my shoulder and breathing sour, smoky fumes into my face. 'Stamford, old chap, I don't suppose you have a spare five hundred or so to get a fellow out of a hole? Just for a while. I mean, I'm good for it.'

'I don't think —' I began, but at that moment Mr French emerged from the office and delivered stony looks at the two of us.

'I need a drink,' said Caldie, and thrusting my empty glass back into my hand, he made a determined path to the bar. I decided that this was a very good time to leave.

CHAPTER SIXTEEN

I did not sleep at all well that night. It was partly due to the disturbing atmosphere at the Wheatsheaf, which was like nothing else I had ever known. I am not entirely sheltered, of course, although my wider education on the ways of the world did not take place in my family home, but in my medical career, where I learned about coarser modes of life and often saw the horrible results. I understood too well what events might happen in such places. It was so different from the easy camaraderie of the King Henry. I knew that there was behaviour there which many might think immoral, but there was no vulgarity, no sense of threat. The Wheatsheaf, for all its pleasanter attractions, was highly unsettling. When I did sleep, I was assailed by the most horrid nightmares which mainly involved Mr French and his cold, piercing eyes.

The following morning, after consuming two large cups of strong coffee, I came to the realisation that Mr Caldie was actually far more afraid of the Wheatsheaf and its managers than I was and knew that I had a duty to inform his sister of what had happened.

I still had her card and walked up to her address in Clerkenwell. It was a bright sunny day, but my mood did not match the weather. On reaching my destination I stood for a while outside a grey apartment building, rehearsing what I was about to say. When I rang the doorbell a lady came to the door, whom I guessed must be Miss Caldie's companion, Miss Mercer. She was unusually thin, her bony fingers stained with ink, and she wore large spectacles with pebble lenses and a gown of severe cut. I suppose I did not look my best, either in my grooming or the neatness of my attire, and she stared at me as if I was a piece of debris someone had deposited on the doorstep.

'I am sorry to intrude,' I said. 'My name is Stamford, and I and my associate Mr Holmes are undertaking some enquiries for Miss Caldie. I don't have an appointment, but I would like, if possible, to speak to Miss Caldie. I have some news concerning her brother.'

This announcement did not improve the nature of Miss Mercer's scrutiny, but after a moment, she said, 'You had better come in. Wait, and I will let her know you are here.'

As I stood in the entrance hall, I did my best to smooth my hair, which I suddenly realised I could not recall having combed that morning, and brushed down my clothes to appear more presentable. It was not many minutes before Miss Mercer reappeared and wordlessly beckoned me to follow.

Miss Caldie occupied a small study where a desk had been placed so that she and Miss Mercer could sit facing each other as they worked. She received me politely, although I could see that my unkempt appearance did not meet with her approval. I was offered a chair and Miss Mercer took a stool and perched silently in one corner.

'So, you have news of my rapscallion brother?' asked Miss Caldie.

'Yes, well, you see, last night I went to see a boxing match at the Wheatsheaf Inn,' I began.

'Are you a boxing man?' she asked. 'You surprise me.' There was no clue in her tone as to whether this was a pleasant surprise or otherwise. I noticed Miss Mercer giving a pout of distaste.

'I — not really, I mean, I take classes in sparring, at another establishment, just for the purpose of exercise. Many respectable gentlemen go there for the same reason. But a boxer I know was matched in a bout at the Wheatsheaf, and I thought I would go to watch, and — um — cheer him on.'

She appeared to accept this explanation. 'Do you attend the Wheatsheaf often? I know it is my brother's frequent haunt. He has never mentioned seeing you there.'

'That was my first visit. And probably my last. I thought it — somewhat unsavoury.'

'So I have been led to believe. Was my brother there?'

'Yes, and we were talking when the landlord, Mr Gough, asked to speak to him. He went into the office and when he came out, he appeared very shocked and frightened and asked to borrow money from me. Five hundred pounds. He must be in some trouble. I thought you ought to know.'

None of these revelations seemed to surprise her. 'Did you lend him any money?'

'No. I have none to lend.'

Miss Caldie paused a long while for thought. I did not interrupt her. 'I appreciate your visit,' she said at last. 'The news you bring is concerning, although not unexpected. You must let me know if you hear anything more. I should mention that Alastair did come to see me late last night. And he was asking for money. I am sure that the five hundred pounds he wanted was not the whole story. I could see that he was afraid. He said there was a creditor who might harm him if he was unable to pay. I think we can guess who that must be.'

'Mr Gough.'

'And he may not be the only one, but if there are others, he will be the worst.'

'Were you able to assist your brother?'

'I refused him, of course. Once one agrees to a loan, it is not the end of the matter. It shows weakness, and he would simply have come back for more. I tasked him about his spendthrift ways and asked him what had happened to the fortune he had inherited from our grandfather. He confessed to me that it had largely gone to pay off his most pressing debts.

'My only offer was to insist that he change his ways. I said that I might be prepared to support him if he showed himself capable of doing honest work. He protested that this arrangement would not suit him, as he needed the funds immediately. I said I was not about to lend him money which I would almost certainly never see again, and he went away.

'I suspect that if one was to look at his status now, he would be considered very nearly bankrupt. Only the Caldie name has enabled him to keep afloat.'

'I believe I understand why his fortunes have changed,' I said. 'The newspaper reports of the accusations against your grandfather, and the possible harm to the Caldie name. I learned very recently that after those reports were published, your brother paid a visit to Charles Smith asking him to withdraw his allegations. Did he tell you he had done so?'

'No, he did not,' she said tartly. 'Without success, I assume.'

'Yes. He must have feared he would no longer be able to get credit.' It occurred to me that humble as my means might be, ironically I might be worth more than Alastair Caldie. 'What do you think can be done for him?'

Miss Caldie gave a dismissive snort. 'He is an adult man. He should be able to decide that for himself,' she declared. 'I have no intention of throwing away my good money on him. I have better uses for it.' I was somewhat startled by this cruel refusal to help her only sibling and it must have shown on my face, for she went on, 'You are not a gambling man, I take it?'

'No, not at all. I have never been tempted. I suppose your brother might be best advised to throw himself on the mercy of Mr Gough. It would be extremely unwise for him to borrow more.'

'Yet that is almost certainly what he will do,' she said. 'I expect that even now he is going the rounds of his disreputable friends, trying to create new debts with which to pay the old ones. I only hope he will not fall into the hands of moneylenders, which would be the fastest way to ruin. In all his life the idea of doing honest work has never occurred to him. It has all been too easy. Until our grandfather's death, we both received allowances from him. There was enough to live on and maintain ourselves respectably, but that was not sufficient for Alastair. I should have seen the signs a year ago, when he became engaged to an heiress. Her father made some enquiries into my brother's means and way of life and put a stop to it. I think we may guess why.'

'He might try that again.'

'He might, but a man in that obvious state of desperation would alarm any prospective father-in-law, not to mention the bride.'

I recalled Holmes's mention of the siblings' widowed mother, who had married an Italian nobleman. 'Perhaps your mother should be informed?' I suggested.

'To what effect? She and her new husband have their own creditors to avoid. They have a title but no money.'

'Then you must be his only hope. Miss Caldie,' I pleaded, 'would you really abandon him? Your own brother?'

She permitted herself one of her rare smiles, a brief moment of warmth. 'He was always my grandfather's favourite. Very well, Mr Stamford, I am persuaded. For my grandfather's sake, and for the family name, I will go and see Alastair and try to make him see sense. At any rate, he must be stopped before he does anything more foolish than he has already.'

I had done my duty and returned home to catch up on my sleep and my studies. The following morning, after a rather better night's rest, I was surprised to receive a note from Miss Caldie. Her brother had not been home for the last two nights, and no-one knew where he was.

CHAPTER SEVENTEEN

My first instinct in the face of this alarming news was to consult Holmes, but he was neither at Barts nor at his rooms in Montague Street. His landlady said he did sleep there, but for the last few days he had been home late and had gone out immediately after breakfast. All I could do was leave him a note. Typically, everyone I asked about his whereabouts seemed to think that I knew more than they did.

I could see that Miss Caldie did have some lingering affection for her wayward brother, but I thought that she was more determined to preserve the family name, her brother's safety being only incidental to that purpose. It had been her concern about the reputation of the Caldie Society, her charitable endeavour, which had prompted her to engage Holmes to discover more about her grandfather's specimen of the great auk.

In Holmes's continued absence I felt therefore that there was something I ought to be doing to pursue this commission, but I could not decide what that might be. Eventually I decided to travel to Kensington to see if Caldie had returned to his home since his sister had written the note I had received that morning.

I found that he was still not at home, and the manservant Mr Duncan, who looked rather drawn and troubled, had no clue to offer as to where his master might be. He asked me my business, and I realised from his manner that he suspected me of being a creditor. I explained that I was simply making enquiries on behalf of Miss Caldie, who was very concerned about her brother, but I was not sure if Duncan believed me. I gave him my card and asked him to let me know as soon as Caldie returned. His response was a despondent sigh.

The Wheatsheaf was conveniently only five minutes' walk away, and so I thought that as I was in the vicinity, I should at least pass it by and observe it. I admit that it was with some trepidation that I approached this hive of illicit activity, which I now knew lurked under a concealing mask of lawful entertainment. The thing I dreaded most was arriving to discover the premises swarming with police, and all the signs of some horrible crime having been committed, most probably with the debt-ridden Caldie as its victim. In fact, all was extremely quiet and untroubled. It was not the busiest time of the day. A glance through a window told me that there were few customers present. I realised that I had an opportunity to go in and take a look about the place while it was less crowded, and perhaps ask some innocent questions about Caldie. He might even be there, pleading for more time to pay his debts, and if so, I would beg him to go and see his sister, who was very concerned for him.

I pushed open the door, entering quietly so as not to draw attention to myself. Knowing that I must appear to be no more than a customer, I sat at a table in the main bar with a modest drink, trying to take an interest in one of the sporting newspapers with which patrons were provided, and hoping that no-one would recognise my efforts to surreptitiously examine the scene.

There was no sign of Alastair Caldie or anyone else I knew. My clandestine sleuthing was not a success, however, since within a minute or two Mr Gough arrived and came to my table, all smiles. 'Welcome again, Mr Stamford!' He sat down, with a breathless tobacco-laden wheeze. 'I am so pleased you could join us again. What is your pleasure?'

'Oh, I just happened to be passing and thought I would come for a rest and a drink,' I said.

He gave me a knowing wink and signalled to the bartender, who promptly began to pour a tankard of ale. It arrived in front of him almost at once. 'Not calling on your friend Mr Caldie, were you? I know he lives very near.' He took a draught of ale and smacked his lips appreciatively.

'Well, no — at least, I did go to his rooms just now, to see him, but his man said he is not at home at present. Have you seen him today?'

'I have not, and I have to admit, that worries me. He is a valued customer. I do hope he is well.'

I was considering whether or not to believe Mr Gough when he leaned towards me confidentially. 'Mr Stamford, I would be most obliged if when you happen to see Mr Caldie again, you would give him a message from me?'

'Oh, yes, of course.'

'Would you be so kind as to let him know that I would like a quiet word. Trivial matter, nothing for him to worry about. Just a quiet word.'

'Yes, I will.'

'I am indebted to you for your assistance,' said Gough appreciatively. The rest of the ale disappeared down his throat. He rose to take his leave but hesitated, as though a thought had just occurred to him. 'I tell you what, Mr Stamford, as we are not too busy right now, why don't I show you around, so you can see what the Wheatsheaf has to offer?'

It seemed like a good opportunity to explore the premises without attracting any suspicion that I might have other motives. Nevertheless, I thought it wise before accepting this invitation to clarify the limited nature of my interests. 'You mean in the way of sporting pursuits?'

'Yes, sporting pursuits,' he said reassuringly. 'Sparring, training, exercise, all the facilities a boxer requires to keep himself up to the mark.'

I agreed, finished my drink, and rose to accompany him. We walked up the stairs, Gough beside me, smiling and patting me cheerfully on the back as if we were old friends. 'I always try to make sure that we have something here to suit everyone,' he said. 'A boxer must train, and all our best men put in a lot of effort, but it is important for them to work their muscles in other ways. We have experts here in Turkish massage, and that is an excellent way to relax and smooth the muscles, and so make them more efficient when action is most needed. It banishes those little strains which inevitably come from hard work. But we also have ways to stimulate the muscles to achieve the powerful bulk in the chest and limbs that all men desire, and all the ladies admire.' This sounded rather advanced to me, but at least it was an improvement on what was offered by the King Henry, which was a rub down with a splash of liniment and a tot of brandy for the pain.

The treatment and exercise room was on the topmost floor. It was smaller than the boxing emporium, but well supplied with dumb-bells and punchbags, and there was a massage table, towels, and a selection of rubbing oils and embrocation. The most unexpected feature was a leather armchair, very well padded, and on a low table beside it a large box of some good quality polished wood. I must have stared at it in curiosity. I suppose my initial thought was that this was a place where boxers could recline if injured and receive treatment, and the box contained medical supplies.

'Ah, I see this has taken your interest,' said Mr Gough. 'This is our comfortable chair, for the ease of our young gladiators when they wish to rest from their labours.' He pressed the upholstered seat to emphasise his comments. 'Would you care to try it out?'

I could hardly refuse, so I sat in the chair.

'All you need to do is lean back, close your eyes, and you will have the most delightful rest,' said Gough. I did as he suggested. 'Oh, and we have some little metal plates that if you put them under the palms of your hands will stimulate the nerves.' I felt some smooth metal slide under my palms. 'Now, how does that feel?'

'It is very pleasant, thank you.' I was about to ask what the metal plates actually did, but before I could speak, I started with surprise, for both my wrists had been seized by some powerful force. I opened my eyes and to my horror I saw that my arms had been fastened to the chair by thick leather straps, firmly buckled, one by Gough, and the other by Mr French, who smiled and cracked his knuckles. I wasn't sure what he was about to do to me, but I felt sure it wasn't a Turkish massage.

'What is happening?' I exclaimed.

'Oh, please don't worry yourself,' said Mr Gough, still the hospitable host. 'You are about to have a trial, quite gratis, of our special muscle enhancer. The straps are for your own safety.' He gestured towards the wooden box. 'Open it up, Mr French.'

The lid of the box was unlatched and lifted. The interior bore a printed label, which announced in large letters, 'Galvani-Electro Muscle Exercise Machine'. Inside I could see a great many coils of black cable, metal tubing, and a brass wheel with a handle.

'By the miracle of electricity, that wondrous fluid which heals all ills, my young boxers are able to develop their muscular strength without so much as getting out of breath,' said Gough. 'Let us have a demonstration.'

There were some fasteners like metal jaws attached to the device by cords which Mr French snapped to the plates under my hands. Before I could protest, another strap secured my ankles.

'Is it safe?' I asked.

'That rather depends on you, Mr Stamford,' said Gough. 'Mr French, turn the wheel.'

'I don't understand. What am I to do?'

'Well, I would recommend you do not struggle, as you may find that any perspiration will only increase the power of the machine.' I was already beginning to perspire, so this was not useful advice. 'And the other thing you could do, is tell me where Mr Alastair Caldie is.'

There was a dull whirring noise as Mr French began to turn the handle and the wheel rotated in a smooth, well-oiled way. At first, I felt nothing and then I sensed a tremor, like a ripple, moving quite gently through the muscles of my arms. Mr French grinned at me.

'I am very sorry, but I don't know where he is,' I said. 'As I told you, I have made enquiries at his home, but he is not there, and his man knows nothing.'

The wheel whirred faster, and my muscles began to twitch, in a way that I did not find at all pleasant.

'Are you quite sure of that, Mr Stamford,' said Gough, 'what with Mr Caldie being a friend of yours? He must owe you money; he owes money to all his friends, so I think you have been keeping a watch on him.'

'He doesn't owe me money, and I don't know where he is,' I protested.

Gough nodded to Mr French, whose powerful shoulders operated without exertion, as if he was part of the machine, and the wheel moved faster still. My arms jerked as if pricked by hundreds of needles and I cried out.

'These machines are said to be very safe for the weakest of persons,' said Mr Gough. 'Of course, someone with a genius for such things might — just might — be able to make some changes the maker did not intend, and the machine will be made to deliver electricity ten times greater than it is supposed to do. Men have been known to faint at the sensation. Mr French here is, I believe, such a genius. He tells me that it is actually possible for the machine to stop a man's heart such that he cannot be revived. And when this man is found deceased, there will be not a mark on him to say how it happened. Now, what do you think of that?'

'I think —' I gasped, 'that Mr Caldie is no friend of mine, and I do not even like him. If I knew where he was, I would gladly tell you, but I do not!'

'Oh, that is very unfortunate,' said Mr Gough. He nodded to his associate.

Mr French had the endurance of an athlete and his face, scarcely expressing any strain from the energy he was expending on the wheel, was stretched very wide by a maniacal grin, showing the most enormous teeth I have ever seen on any man, while little points of light shone in his steely eyes.

I tried to wrench my arms free, but they were firmly pressed to the metal plates. I don't know if it was real or my imagination, but the twitching seemed to be spreading down my body. I really thought I was about to die. My only hope was to make up some lie my captors might believe, and I tried frantically to devise something to say.

At this moment the door flew open, and a figure stood there. Hope leaped in my chest. I tried to speak but could utter only gasps. I thought it must be Holmes come to rescue me but saw at once that it was not. The new arrival appeared to be a cook, or at least the figure was small and female, and her gown was enveloped in a voluminous and well-worn apron.

'How did you get in here? Back to the kitchen with you!' ordered Gough, but she did not stir. That was when I saw that she wore steel-rimmed spectacles and was holding a gun.

'Allow me to introduce myself,' she said, casting aside the apron. 'I am Emmeline Caldie, sister of Alastair. I believe you have been trying to locate him.'

'Well now,' said Gough, 'that being the case, perhaps you would like to tell me where he is.' He signalled to Mr French to halt his efforts. My tormentor, with every sign of reluctance, allowed the wheel to slow down and stop. I lay there and panted for breath, as if I had just run a race.

'I am sorry to say I don't know where my brother is, and neither does Mr Stamford,' said Miss Caldie. 'However, I am here to offer you a compromise. You must agree to release Mr Stamford unharmed. You must also promise not to harm my brother should you be able to find him. For my part, if you let me have a full account of his debts, I will do my best to locate him and see to it that he pays you in full.'

'How do we know that you will keep your promise?' demanded Gough. 'I have had promises like that before, and hardly anyone keeps them.'

'I am asking you to accept the word of a lady,' said Miss Caldie. 'If you are unable to do so, I am afraid I will be obliged to shoot someone. I should mention that while my brother did not inherit our grandfather's celebrated skill with guns, I did.'

'Well, well, well,' said Mr Gough. He gave an unexpected bark of a laugh. 'I'll say this, it's almost worth it to let this little fish go since I have had the pleasure of meeting you. Your brother has told me you are worth a good deal; in fact, he often complains you won't share your wealth with him. So at least one member of the family is good for the money.' He hummed, thoughtfully. 'All right, we have an agreement. Mr French, release Mr Stamford.' The straps were undone, and I stumbled from the chair, rubbing the pain from my arms.

'Come over here,' ordered Miss Caldie.

My legs could hardly hold me up, but I was able to reach her. Her aim held steady as she handed me a card. 'Give this to Mr Gough.'

Although I had no wish to approach that gentleman again, I obeyed. Mr Gough gave a mocking bow as he took the card from me. I retreated to the side of my rescuer as quickly as I was able.

After reading the card, Gough held it to his nose with a salacious expression, as if hoping to detect a feminine scent, before putting it in his pocket. 'I wish you good day,' he said.

Miss Caldie remained wary and maintained her guard. 'And now we will take our leave,' she said. 'You first, Mr Stamford, and I will follow.' To my immense relief, Mr Gough and Mr French made no attempt to prevent our departure. I was directed to the servant's stairs, and by way of the kitchen and pantry we soon found ourselves outside. There was a hansom cab waiting in the street. Miss Caldie bundled me into it and took a seat, snapping out an order to the driver to proceed.

As we began to move, she looked at me searchingly. 'Are you about to faint? I might have to strike you if you do. It is not my habit to carry smelling salts.'

I muttered something to the effect that I would do my best to remain conscious. I made a great effort to thank her in suitable terms, but she waved this aside and ordered me to cease.

'You are a poor specimen of a man,' she said, 'but at least you are honest.'

I was unable to disagree on either count. 'What brought you to the Wheatsheaf?' I asked.

'Most probably the same as you. I was looking for my brother. But it is clear to me now that he is not there. I saw you go in and when you did not emerge, I thought I would see if you had encountered any difficulties. Naturally I could not go in as a customer. Respectable women are not advised to frequent such a place, but I was able to enter the kitchen and by adopting a disguise, I masqueraded as a cook.'

'Was the door to that awful room not locked?' I asked.

'It was, but the kitchen is supplied with trussing needles.'

When I came to reflect on this incident much later, it did occur to me that Miss Caldie was as well-equipped as any man to be a detective, an occupation she appeared disinclined to pursue. 'Do you think you can find your brother?' I asked.

'I believe so. He has the curious qualities of being both erratic and predictable. I shall make the appropriate enquiries.'

The cab deposited me outside the door of my rooms. I tried to thank her again, but my words were drowned by the sound of the horse's hooves as it moved away.

CHAPTER EIGHTEEN

I will not describe the miserable night I spent following that horrible ordeal. The experience was to haunt my waking hours and invade my dreams for many years to come. Next morning, I somehow managed to rise wearily from my rumpled bed, make myself moderately presentable and venture out. The fresh air did me some good as I walked to Barts, hoping that Holmes might have returned.

I was relieved to find him at his bench in the laboratory, setting up a new experiment. The gas burners were blazing and there was an acrid waft of chemicals in the air. He looked to be his usual self, although he instantly saw signs about me that I had not had a restful few days in his absence. 'Whatever have you been about, Stamford?' he demanded. 'Are you ill?' When I made some stammering attempt at describing the ghastly episode, he at once abandoned his work, took me to a quiet corner of a nearby hostelry, and bought me a brandy to steady my nerves.

Holmes appeared to be perfectly at his ease with his pipe and his beer as he waited for me to tell my tale. He listened attentively as I described my two visits to the Wheatsheaf and what had transpired there. His expression did not change until I told him of my predicament with the galvanism machine, and Miss Caldie's dramatic arrival, when I saw his eyebrows rise, and a little smile play at the corners of his mouth. I have to admit I was just a little offended, as I could not see anything remotely humorous about the situation.

'I do not find that lady's company very congenial, but it was extremely welcome at that point,' I added.

'I take it you escaped without injury,' he said.

'Yes, although I dread to think what might have happened if my rescuer had not found me,' I said, shuddering at the memory of Mr French's staring eyes, horrible teeth, and the vigorous movement of his shoulder as he turned the crank.

'Perhaps they thought the mere threat would produce the result they wanted,' Holmes observed, 'since I rather doubt the machine would actually do what they suggested.'

I must admit I had never thought of that and felt even more foolish than I already did, if that were possible.

'But it sounds to me as if Miss Caldie has come to a suitable arrangement in the absence of her brother, and you are most unlikely to be troubled again,' said Holmes.

I finished my brandy and contemplated another, but I did not think it would do me any good. 'And you must have been busy, Holmes,' I said, 'to be absent for so long.' If he detected a note of rebuke in my voice, he did not respond to it.

'I have, and you will be pleased to know that I have made something of an advance in my enquiries regarding the murder of Mr Smith,' he said. 'Lestrade has confirmed that the police have found no trace of any cabman who might have taken Smith to Bishopsgate, from which it is assumed that the victim must have walked. I have been exploring the probable routes he took, of which there are several, and visiting the tobacconists on the way where he might have called to renew his stock of pipe tobacco. Since he had in the last fifteen years acquired a slight antipodean accent, that was the main means by which he might have been remembered, although the proximity to a shipping company office selling passages to New Zealand did rather hamper my efforts. By this means I discovered one promising lead. I was told of a man who met Smith's description asking a tobacconist about the very brand we knew he smoked, one they did not stock. The man was unaccompanied, and there I thought the trail might end, but I left my card in case they could recall anything more, and yesterday this was rewarded. A young assistant who had not been present at the time of my visit had been told of it, and he remembered something of interest. I went to interview him.'

Holmes paused to refill his pipe before he went on. It was certainly a promising development, but I felt too exhausted to fully appreciate his efforts at creating anticipation. 'He had been working on the window display when the man we believe to be Smith entered the shop. He did not notice Smith especially but as he worked, he saw a man standing outside, who appeared to be taking a great interest in the display. He thought to identify what product had engaged the man's attention, but on closer observation, he realised that he was not looking at the items arranged in the window but through them, at something inside the shop. He rather thought the man was staring at Smith. The assistant continued with his work, but as Smith left the shop, he saw the watcher hold back, as if he did not wish to be seen. After a few moments, the man pulled his hat down over his eyes and followed Smith. The assistant thought it highly peculiar; in fact, he wondered if the customer was a criminal and the watcher a plain clothes policeman or detective. He asked the other assistants about the customer and was told only that he was from New Zealand and had been asking about Cameron's tobacco.'

'Could he describe the man following Smith?'

'Young, active, respectably dressed, beardless, nothing to make him stand out as remarkable. Had he been a detective, he might well have chosen to appear like any man in a crowd so as not to be noticed.'

'Do you think,' I said, 'that he might have been Alastair Caldie? He had already tried unsuccessfully to make Smith withdraw his allegation, and I saw how desperate he had become. Perhaps he wanted to talk to him again and it became violent. Smith might have lost his temper, and Caldie retaliated.'

'Caldie might lash out if he were attacked,' mused Holmes. 'He has seen enough boxing to think he knows what to do. But as for the rest — well, I might have misjudged him, I suppose. A man facing ruin will sometimes find reserves he did not know he possessed.'

'Or Caldie might have got one of his boxing friends to do what he dared not do,' I said.

Holmes leaned back in his chair and puffed thoughtfully on his pipe. I waited for his observation and at last he said, 'I know many pugilists who in their private lives would put to shame men who like to think of themselves as gentlemen. But there are some who, for need or love of money, are little more than bullies for hire. They may not always use force, sometimes the threat of it is enough to intimidate, but they will if necessary. And a man who is trained to use his fists — with those fists hardened against blows and pain — will find them to be his best weapons. I cannot imagine a pugilist picking up a piece of wood to attack a man from behind or throttling him when he had him down. I could be wrong, of course. A man whose hands are weakened by injury or age might resort to a weapon, but the man who followed Smith was young.'

'Perhaps Brandon Molloy could tell us something about Caldie and his associates?' I suggested. 'He was boxing at the Wheatsheaf, and I think he has fought there before.'

'Yes,' agreed Holmes. 'I must speak to him. There is more than one reason why I might like to know a great deal more about Alastair Caldie.'

It was not difficult to arrange a meeting with Molloy. Holmes thought it best to select a hostelry not frequented by the boxing fraternity in order to encourage freedom of conversation. Molloy was about twenty-three. He was doing well as a young professional while remaining careful to abide by the rules which enabled him to stay within the law. He boxed at a number of venues where there was often a riotous crowd of young men who liked drinking and gambling and supported the careers of their favourites. Unlike many pugilists who gathered great wealth only to lose it again, Molloy's ambition was to accumulate enough funds from his winnings to go into business and raise a family. Molloy, of course, remembered Holmes as a student of Professor Logan at the King Henry and had seen Holmes acquit himself with distinction when sparring.

'Mr Caldie is a man who talks more than he does,' said Molloy, as he quenched his thirst with a foaming ale, 'and I have learned to be wary of him. I have been told he hosts gatherings at his apartment for his sporting friends where there are actresses and gentlemen gamblers and their bullies, and there is a lot of strong drink and all sorts of goings-on. Not that I would attend such things. I have a young lady I wish to marry, and she is worth ten of any woman I have ever met.'

'You say he talks more than he does,' said Holmes. 'What does he talk about?'

'Oh, all the money he got from his grandfather, and also he complains about his sister — well, it's not a nice thing to say, but — he says her purse strings are tighter than her stays. He thinks she ought to marry and have a full nursery so there is something to take her mind off all her other nonsense.'

We said nothing, although I suspect we were both thinking there was little chance of that.

'Did he ever mention a Mr Smith?' asked Holmes.

Molloy laughed. 'Yes, well, he told us a tale not long ago. He was at the Wheatsheaf, drinking as usual, and he talked about what a villain called Smith did at the museum — something about him attacking a stuffed bird with a hammer, and what an insult it was to his grandfather, not that I could work out what it had to do with his grandfather — and how he would gladly give £50 to any man who would punch Smith in the head for him, to teach him a lesson.'

'Do you know if anyone took him up on that offer?' asked Holmes, calmly.

'Not in public, not right then, but of course private arrangements can be made. Some of the boxing men earn most of their money by working as bodyguards or keeping order at clubs, when they don't have any bouts arranged, so it wouldn't be an unusual thing for them to use their fists outside of the ring.'

'What bouts took place on the day you mention?' asked Holmes.

'It was the annual championships of the West London Boxing Club,' said Molloy. 'There was a big crowd.'

'I assume that pressmen were there in force to report on the meeting?'

'Oh yes, it was in all the sporting papers, and the local press as well.'

Holmes said nothing, but after we had bid Molloy goodbye, he commented, 'It is more than possible that a pressman might have overheard young Caldie's accusations. I think we can now guess how the story reached the newspapers, and it was not through Smith.'

'Are you going to let the museum know?'

'I will, of course, although there is little point in doing so. But it is a line the police will not have pursued, so I will make sure that Lestrade learns of it. Even if Caldie did not intentionally hire a man to punish Smith, his words might unwittingly have instigated the fatal attack on the turbulent ornithologist. The delivery yard of a public house is not such an exalted place as Canterbury Cathedral, but the implications are the same. Caldie, if he is ever found, will no doubt deny everything.'

Holmes tapped out his pipe and consulted his watch. 'But now it is high time for me to arrange another interview with Professor Beare and Dr Woodley. I hope at last to be permitted to view that curious label which they conspired to conceal from the world.'

CHAPTER NINETEEN

On the following day Holmes informed me that he had been granted permission to see the label that had been removed from the base of the questionable exhibit of the great auk.

We met with Professor Beare and Dr Woodley in their office at the museum, and this time I saw a stiff card envelope lying on the desk. It had been placed just beyond our reach and very near to Professor Beare's fingertips, as though he might like to snatch it away should he change his mind.

The two gentlemen greeted us and asked if we had made any progress in our enquiries.

'I have spoken to Mr and Miss Caldie, who have been extremely helpful and provided me with their grandfather's papers, including his diaries. I learned that Sir Andrew Caldie occasionally gave lectures to members of the Edinburgh University ornithological society about the collection and preservation of birds. From time to time he received specimens from students, and other persons who knew of his interests. In his diaries I can find no record of his collecting or receiving a specimen of the great auk. I do not believe he ever went to St Kilda. In 1855, however, he received a visitor, from whom he purchased a badly preserved skin of *Alca torda*, a razorbill from that island. I have not been able to discover what, if anything, he did with it.'

'Did he name the visitor?' asked Dr Woodley.

'Regrettably, he did not.'

'Surely you are not suggesting that what we have is a partial skin of a razorbill?' asked Beare. 'I can assure you, there is nothing of that bird in our exhibit.'

'I make no such suggestion,' said Holmes. 'I do not have the expertise to make that distinction and rely entirely upon your guidance. Before I continue, I must ask if you have made any enquiries of your own which have uncovered any new information? You must be open with me, even if you feel you need to protect another individual.'

Professor Beare sighed deeply. 'We have nothing more to tell you,' he said. 'And our first duty as always is to protect the birds, creatures which have never harmed another soul. When I petitioned Parliament for a law to prevent the killing of seabirds, I was accused of being sentimental. Those men who went by the boatload to shoot gulls in their thousands for sport, saw me as a soft-hearted fool who wanted to interfere with their natural right to take pleasure in the destruction of life. They think that the birds will always be there for their guns. After all, they said, in America, the passenger pigeon numbers many millions, and hunting does not seem to diminish their numbers. Fortunately, we were able to show that seabirds are of value to man, since their cries signal to vessels in poor weather that land is near. It swayed Parliament, and the Act became law. But is sentiment such a bad thing? I own to it; I am proud of it. Can we not preserve our feathered friends in the wild, out of sentiment, rather than seek some use they might have? We should strive to be more sentimental, more compassionate. I would not willingly protect any man who destroys life for his own amusement.'

Dr Woodley gazed upon his mentor with undisguised filial affection for the old man. 'My feelings precisely,' he said.

'But if you would now be so kind as to allow me to see the label?' said Holmes.

Beare murmured agreement, and with great care he opened the envelope, withdrew a rather soiled square of paper, and laid it on the desk. 'The ink has faded somewhat,' he said regretfully, 'and I admit the writing is not entirely clear; however, my examination suggests that my reading of it is correct.' He took a magnifying glass from the desk drawer and passed it over the label, then nodded, and slid it closer to us. 'You may examine it, gentlemen, but please, I beg of you, do not touch it.'

Holmes took his own glass from his pocket and spent some moments in study, then handed it to me for a look. The label was a thin sheet of plain paper, unmarked apart from the handwriting. Although a little faded, perhaps from the quality of the ink used, the wording was clear enough: 'Great Auk. St Kilda, 1855'. There was a small smear of ink in the lower right corner, perhaps where a drop had fallen and been blotted. I saw Holmes pay special attention to it. 'Gentlemen, would you permit me to take this item to my laboratory for a further examination under better light?' he asked.

Neither of the two authorities looked content with that suggestion. 'I rather think it ought to remain here,' said Woodley.

Beare hesitated, then picked up the label and replaced it in the envelope. 'Due to the sensitive nature of the item, I regret I cannot allow it to leave my possession,' he said. 'Of course, I trust you, but accidents may occur.' He returned the envelope to the drawer of his desk and turned a key in the lock.

Holmes received this decision with surprising equanimity. 'Do either of you recognise the handwriting on the label?' he asked.

'I am afraid not,' said Woodley. 'I assume it must be that of Sir Andrew Caldie. But as we know, a man's handwriting may change over twenty or more years.'

'That is true,' agreed Holmes. 'The handwriting is either that of Sir Andrew or the manservant who assisted him, who is unfortunately deceased. I doubt it will tell us anything.'

Both gentlemen appeared to accept that conclusion.

'Have you been able to confirm if it was Smith who went to the newspapers?' asked Beare.

'I have found no proof that he did,' said Holmes. 'His mother said he did not, and he was very angry when he saw what was published. She was not, however, aware of all his business and correspondence. It is possible that he wrote a scholarly letter which was ignored. But the story in the press was not the one he would have told. No, the culprit, I feel sure was Mr Alastair Caldie who, when in his cups, inveighed against Mr Smith for tarnishing his grandfather's name. He was with his friends at a boxing match where men of the popular press were present, and I think he must have been overheard. It was not intentional, and he may have no recollection of the incident.'

Woodley and Beare exchanged glances with weary sighs at the profligacy of youth. 'Well, I must thank you for clarifying that mystery at least,' said Beare.

'But I have something to ask you,' Holmes continued. 'The late Mr Smith hinted to an associate and in a letter to me that he thought he knew where and when the specimen to which he took such exception was collected. Not only that, but he suspected who it was who collected it. But he declined to say any more, as he required proof. As far as I am aware, Smith never saw the label mentioning St Kilda; however, Mrs Smith, to whom I was able to speak recently, told me that her son had been talking about making a visit to St Kilda before his return to New Zealand. I must ask you, gentlemen — did Smith ever see the label or anything else that hinted at the origin of the specimen? Do you know where he obtained that information?'

'He never saw the label as far as I am aware,' said Beare. 'It has been under lock and key since the exhibit was received by the museum.'

'I am sure he never saw it,' said Woodley, confidently.

'Did Smith ever write to the museum?' asked Holmes. 'I believe he was planning to, and his mother told me he wrote more than one letter on the same day he wrote to me. If so, I feel sure he did not address it to Professor Owen, who has ignored all the others, so I expect he must have written it to you.'

Professor Beare was silent for a moment, then he nodded, sadly. 'I received a letter from him, yes. It included a repeat of the accusations he had made at the unveiling and said that he was planning to go to St Kilda, although he did not say what he hoped to do there. I was about to write to him to dissuade him from this scheme. The last thing I wanted was questions being asked which would send collectors to the island. I was hoping to arrange a meeting to discuss his complaints when Mrs Smith arrived very distressed, saying her son was missing and asking me if I had seen him. I said that as far as I knew he had not visited the museum on any day since the unveiling. I certainly had not seen him since that unhappy incident. Had you, Woodley?'

'No. Neither had I received a letter from him,' said Woodley.

'I have to admit,' continued Beare, 'that my first thought, which was rather upsetting, was that Smith had already departed for St Kilda and there was nothing I could do about it. I tried to reassure Mrs Smith, saying that if he had gone on a trip then he would surely write to her with all the details. I asked her to let me know as soon as she heard from him. But she would not be comforted. She was adamant that he would never have gone away on such a long journey without telling her first. And then, of course, we heard the horrible news. Has there been any progress? Have the police arrested anyone?'

'Not yet,' said Holmes. His tone was not so much an admission of defeat but a solemn promise.

Holmes and I walked back to Barts. A thought had been forming in my mind during the interview and I now expressed it. 'Holmes, you know of course that I am making a special study of ophthalmology in addition to my general classes?'

'I do.'

'I noticed that Professor Beare found the handwriting on the label harder to read than we did. I watched him very carefully when he used the magnifying glass, and I saw it was simply to enable him to read rather than make a detailed study as you do. I tried as far as I was able to observe his eyes. I saw no obvious clouding, no signs of cataracts. But a man of his age might well have some atrophy of the retina, which is not apparent in an external examination, and which could cause blurred vision.'

Holmes considered my comments. 'Do you mean that when examining the label and the exhibit, Professor Beare might have seen what he hoped to see, and Woodley does not want to contradict him out of loyalty and regard?'

'That is possible, yes.'

'It is clear that Professor Beare most urgently did not want Smith to go to St Kilda.'

'But I cannot imagine he would have done anything desperate to prevent him,' I said. 'And we know that Dr Woodley doesn't even think there is a colony to protect.'

'I would dearly like to identify the man whose writing is on the label,' said Holmes. 'All I can say at present is that despite the speculation about how handwriting alters with age, it is not that of Sir Andrew Caldie. But there is something else on the label which is partially hidden under the ink smear. It may be a mere nothing, the kind of marking a man makes simply to test the nib of his pen, or it might prove to be a palpable clue. But my glass is not powerful enough to show it in sufficient detail.'

'Is that why you were hoping to take it to the laboratory?'

'It is, but I have a plan to achieve my ends,' said Holmes. I must have looked worried, for he smiled. 'Have no fear, it does not involve burglary. That is a skill I have yet to acquire.'

I decided not to mention Miss Caldie's dexterity with the trussing needle.

CHAPTER TWENTY

Our next meeting with Miss Caldie to report on our progress in the case of her grandfather's great auk was looming uncomfortably near. I had not set eyes on her since she had driven me home after my encounter with the effects of galvanism, and I was somewhat concerned as to how she would behave towards me. I need not have worried, as she made no reference to the event and was as cool in her manner as ever.

We saw her at her apartments in Clerkenwell, where she received us in the drawing room. This was a generously sized room furnished with the kind of seating more appropriate to a library, handsome yet practical lamps, and a great many books. I saw Holmes making a careful survey of the contents of the shelves. I followed his gaze and observed some venerable leather-bound volumes, some of which, from the ornamental stamping on the spines, appeared to be on the subject of birds. I recalled Miss Caldie saying that this was a subject in which she had no great interest and guessed that these were from the collection of her grandfather. It appeared that in the division of the estate, the son had chosen to house the hunting guns and the daughter the books.

Miss Mercer was also present. I had received the strong impression that she was to Miss Caldie as I was to Holmes, a trusted, loyal, and biddable assistant. Miss Mercer and I eyed each other across the room, and I believe an understanding of our situation may have passed between us.

'I have made some progress in the search for my brother,' announced Miss Caldie. 'His manservant, Mr Duncan, who appears extremely reluctant to say anything on the subject, has revealed to me that Alastair borrowed a few pounds from him and left his apartments carrying a small travelling bag. I have since established that he purchased a railway ticket which will take him as far as Scotland. Our family has a few small properties there still, about which I suspect Mr Gough almost certainly knows nothing. I have sent some telegrams and employed agents to make enquiries. My plan is, when Alastair has been found, to arrange for a payment to placate Mr Gough. Since my brother cannot be trusted with money, I believe the best course of action would be to engage a solicitor to arrange a transfer of Alastair's share of a small parcel of land to me. I will then sell it and pay the debt.'

'Do you think he will agree to that?' I asked.

'I shall make it very clear to him that the alternatives are far worse. It will leave my brother with almost nothing, but it can't be helped.'

'He will have the Caldie name,' I ventured.

'Yes, although in some respects that has been his downfall. He has drawn upon it too lavishly.'

'I wish you every success,' said Holmes. 'A brother is so frequently the most troubling member of the family.' I wondered how Holmes knew this, as he had not mentioned any brother to me, but his expression told me nothing.

'Thank you,' said Miss Caldie. 'But tell me, how have your enquiries progressed?'

'I have made a thorough examination of your grandfather's papers, which mainly detail his travels in the tropics, but I have not found any reference to the great auk,' said Holmes. 'If he ever acquired a specimen, it can only have come from northern latitudes. The British Museum has one from the Orkney Islands.'

'I am sure he never went there,' said Miss Caldie.

'He might have purchased one from another collector,' said Holmes. 'However, I find it surprising given the rarity of the item that he never recorded such an acquisition in his diary. Perhaps there was something in the nature of that purchase he wished to conceal. The only person who might have advised me is his late servant, Mr McCaskie. Can you think of anyone else I can consult?'

Miss Caldie gave this some thought. 'My housekeeper Mrs McGillivray worked very devotedly for my grandfather during the last fifteen years of his life. She has been made aware of my current concerns, and I have asked her about his collections, but it seems she never assisted him in his preparation of the specimens. Also, he did less work of that nature in those years than formerly due to declining health, and very little in the last five.'

'I would like to speak to her,' said Holmes. 'She might recall something Mr McCaskie said which would advance my enquiries.'

'Of course,' said Miss Caldie. She rang for the housekeeper, who appeared before us shortly afterwards. Mrs McGillivray was a burly individual of about forty, who looked equal to commanding any household with efficiency and decorum.

'Mrs McGillivray, these gentlemen are seeking to exonerate my late grandfather from the deplorable suggestion of fraud which has been made against him recently. Please answer any questions they may ask you.'

'Yes, Miss Caldie,' said the housekeeper. She had a firm voice and broad Scots accent.

'I shall retire to my study. Miss Mercer, I will require your assistance.' Miss Mercer said nothing but rose to her feet. Miss Caldie left us, with her shadow following.

'Please take a seat,' said Holmes, who liked to put people at their ease, and after a moment's hesitation, Mrs McGillivray did as he suggested. 'My name is Sherlock Holmes, and this is my associate Mr Stamford. We are not ornithologists, but we study chemistry and anatomy at Barts, and have in the past given assistance to the British Museum in their endeavours. We have been granted permission to examine Sir Andrew Caldie's papers, and I am hoping you might be able to assist us.'

'I will do whatever I can to help you, gentlemen,' said Mrs McGillivray. 'Sir Andrew was a good man and a good master, and I would not have his name brought into disrepute.'

'The item that has been called into question,' Holmes continued, 'is a specimen of the flightless bird, the great auk, which he bequeathed to the British Museum. Do you recall it?'

'I am not sure,' replied the housekeeper. 'There were always displays of stuffed birds around the house, but I am not an expert to tell one from another. Can you describe it?'

'Perhaps a book might help us,' I suggested.

Holmes nodded agreement. 'Please fetch one,' he said.

I examined the venerable volumes on the bookshelf, most of which referred to the birds of the Americas, which I recalled were Sir Andrew's special interest. More promising was Thomas Bewick's *History of British Birds*, an edition published in 1809, a time when, so I had learned, the great auk was still an occasional visitor. Fortunately, it included not only a description but also an engraving of the great auk, which I showed to the housekeeper.

'Ah, yes, the big penguin, as I used to think of it, though Sir Andrew was always at great pains to say it was no such thing,' she said with a smile. 'I do remember it, as it was so unusual.'

'Where did he keep the specimen?'

'In his study in a glass case.'

'Did Sir Andrew tell you anything about how or when he acquired it?' asked Holmes. 'In fact, did you ever see him working on it?'

The housekeeper shook her head emphatically. 'No, he never told me where it came from, and I was never to go into his workshop. He said there were powders and suchlike in there that he wanted to keep under lock and key, as they might be harmful, and it was better if I didn't touch them. The only time I ever helped him was when he asked me to dust the poor things. He had a very fine brush he liked to use, but when he was older his hands would shake, and he thought it was better if I did it.'

'Did you ever see any label on the great auk specimen? It might have had one on the base.'

'It might, but all I ever did was dust it.'

'Sir Andrew's butler, Mr McCaskie, used to assist him in his workshop, I believe?'

'He did, yes.'

'He never imparted anything to you about the specimen?'

'No, and I never enquired. But he was a very knowledgeable man. In fact, he was something of a chemist himself. I still use his recipe for silver polish. None better.'

'After Mr McCaskie's death, did Sir Andrew employ another assistant?'

'No. There were young gentlemen from the university who used to come sometimes to study his methods, and they gave him what assistance he needed.'

Holmes was examining the volume. 'Even when this was published the species was not numerous,' he observed. 'It says "seldom seen on the British shores," although there is a mention of where they are occasionally found.' He tapped the page with a long finger and showed it to me, and I saw a reference to St Kilda. Then something caught Holmes's eye and he started abruptly, a quizzical furrow in his brow. 'Hm,' he said, then after a few moments the frown was replaced by an expression of almost beatific clarity.

Mrs McGillivray waited, but whatever had produced Holmes's exclamation he chose not to elaborate. 'I would be obliged if you could let me see Mr McCaskie's recipe for silver polish,' he said. 'Unless it is a secret, of course.'

'Oh, no, I can show it to you now if you wish.'

'Please do.'

Mrs McGillivray left us, and I asked Holmes what he had seen in the book. It was open at the page on the great auk, and he passed it to me without a word. I read the article very carefully, which referred to the bird being found in Norway and Iceland, as well as the Faroes, but nothing struck me as especially remarkable. The readers of this memoir will think me singularly obtuse, and I invite them to examine a copy of the volume for themselves, to see if they can detect what called itself to Holmes's sudden attention. I was about to ask him to enlighten me when Mrs McGillivray returned.

The housekeeper had brought a small notebook, which she passed to Holmes. 'This was Mr McCaskie's,' she said. 'He wrote all his recipes in there, which I have found very helpful.'

Holmes glanced through the little book and made careful notes in his pocketbook before handing it back. 'He had very neat handwriting,' he observed.

'Oh yes, he was always very meticulous about that.' She hesitated, then said, 'Mr Holmes, you said that you were both chemists.'

'That is one subject of our studies, yes.'

'I was wondering if you could advise me.' She drew something from her pocket. It was a small paper bag, from which she extracted a medicine bottle. 'It's been troubling me for a while, and I didn't know who to go to for the best.'

CHAPTER TWENTY-ONE

Holmes took the bottle from the housekeeper and held it up for examination. It was a six-ounce clear glass medicine bottle, bearing the printed label of a nearby pharmacy. The contents were stated to be a general calming mixture, one teaspoonful to be taken three times a day. The patient was Miss Caldie, and it was dated the previous December. The bottle was filled very nearly to the shoulders, showing that very little of the medicine had been taken.

'Miss Caldie mentioned to me that she and her brother had both been taken ill last winter,' said Holmes. 'Is this relating to that illness?'

'Yes, and that was such a curious thing,' said Mrs McGillivray. 'We never did discover what the matter was, and it was put down to some bad fish, although I am not at all sure that was the case. I think,' she said, drawing herself up a little, 'I can tell the difference between a fresh and a bad fish before I cook it. And that one was as plump and bright-eyed a fish as I have ever seen from the market.'

'I would appreciate it if you would tell me more about the meal at which this fish was served,' said Holmes. 'I might be able to resolve the mystery.'

'I would be very grateful if you could. It has worried me ever since.'

'Omit nothing, however trivial,' said Holmes, leaning back expectantly in his chair. 'Start with the purpose of the gathering. Was it to mark a special occasion?'

'Not that I know of. Mr Caldie was to call on his sister to have dinner, as he said there was a business matter which he wished to discuss with her. It was about two months after Sir Andrew died and the estate was still being settled, although if the truth be known, it was Miss Caldie who did most of the work.'

'You surprise me,' said Holmes, drily.

'Yes, well, Mr Caldie had his man go to the market and buy a nice fish for the dinner, and have it sent here. Miss Caldie is very partial to fish, as she says it is good for the brain. I received the fish, which looked very good and fresh, and I poached it in milk, which I used to make a white sauce. Miss Mercer was to dine with them, but she does not like the taste of fish, so I made her an egg with a lemon sauce. There were the same vegetables for all, and a pudding.'

'And both brother and sister were afflicted?'

'Yes, they were.'

'What about Miss Mercer?'

'She was not. That was the reason we thought it must be the fish.'

Holmes and I exchanged a glance at that point, and I believe we were both thinking the same thing.

'Can you describe the symptoms?' I asked. 'When did they begin?'

'It must have been about a quarter of an hour after the meal began. There was a great deal of discussion at the table, and the pudding had not yet been served. The first sign was that Miss Caldie complained of pains in the stomach and feeling very sick. Then Mr Caldie said he was feeling bilious. Eventually Miss Caldie retired to her bedroom, and Miss Mercer went to see to her. She was not at all well. I found that Miss Mercer did not know what to do in the circumstances, but I had heard that the best thing in such cases is to wash the stomach with a good quantity of liquid. So I went and fetched some broth and new milk, and made Miss Caldie drink it all, which she was not at all willing to do. It was not a pleasant business for anyone, but it did bring her some relief. Mr Caldie, meanwhile, had gone into the water closet in something of a hurry. I spoke to him through the door, and he said he would attend to his own requirements. When he came out, he was holding a handkerchief over his face and pressing on his stomach, which he said pained him a great deal. Then he came to see me and said that the fish must have been bad, and if there was any left over, I had better throw it away. I wanted to call a doctor, but he thought he should take a cab home while he still felt able, so his man could look after him.'

'So,' said Holmes, 'the fish was eaten by Mr and Miss Caldie, but Miss Mercer, who was unaffected, did not partake. What of the vegetables?'

'I think everyone at the table partook of that dish.'

'And the milk?'

'I used some for the fish and the rest for Miss Mercer's lemon sauce.'

'Were there drinks served?'

'Mr Caldie brought a bottle of wine, and he had at least two or three glasses. Miss Caldie and Miss Mercer had a glass each. There was mineral water on the table, but I couldn't say for certain who drank any, although I suspect the ladies had some, but not Mr Caldie. Miss Caldie also had her tisane, which she prefers to wine.'

'You are saying that the only item which was consumed solely by Mr and Miss Caldie was the fish? Is that correct?'

There was a long silence. 'The thing is, Mr Holmes,' said Mrs McGillivray, hesitantly, 'the fish in sauce had been sent back to the kitchen, very nearly all of it consumed, but there was a little left, and I admit I took a piece of bread to it and made it my supper. I do not approve of waste.'

'And did you have any symptoms?'

'No, none. I can only think that the amount I had was too little to affect me, and I do have a strong stomach.'

'And this mixture,' said Holmes, holding up the medicine bottle. 'It was prescribed by Miss Caldie's doctor?'

'Yes, Miss Mercer ran to fetch him, and when he called he agreed that the fish must be at fault, and she only wanted rest and strengthening. Miss Caldie took a dose but when she did, she felt worse than before. The sickness started up again, and there were other symptoms I won't describe. I had to wash her stomach again. I told her she ought not to have any more, and she agreed; in fact, she told me to throw it away. But I thought I ought to go back to the chemist, as I was worried there was something in the mixture that disagreed with her. He assured me it was the gentlest possible soothing remedy, suitable for the very young, and ladies of a delicate constitution. All the same, he gave me another bottle and I brought it home, and when Miss Caldie had a dose of that, it did her good.'

'But you kept this one. Why was that?'

'There was something that had sunk to the bottom of the bottle. A kind of white powder. I don't know what it is. And there was none present in the new one. I made sure of that before Miss Caldie took any. That was when I thought, if there was ever to be some kind of official enquiry, perhaps into the chemist's shop, it could be looked at. Maybe it wasn't in the medicine at all, but something bad had got into the bottle.'

Holmes held the bottle up to the light and we both looked at it closely.

'It is not so visible, now,' said Mrs McGillivray, 'as it might have dissolved somewhat, but I decided not to disturb it, and there should be enough to examine. I have had no-one to go to for advice, and it would be a bad thing to accuse a professional man without proof. He has a new assistant, and I did think maybe it wasn't the chemist but that young man who made a mistake. But if you could look at it, I would be so grateful. It may turn out to be nothing, which would put my mind at rest.'

'Who went to the chemist for this bottle?'

'Miss Mercer.'

'Was that on the same day the doctor called?'

'Yes, that evening, just after he had gone.'

'And when it was brought home, where was it kept?'

'On the nightstand beside Miss Caldie's bed.'

'And she took the first dose then?'

'No. We were instructed not to give it until she was able to keep down food. She was unwell for several hours and then finally fell asleep. She was resting peacefully, so we didn't like to disturb her.'

'Did anyone watch over Miss Caldie during the night?'

'Yes, Miss Mercer slept in a chair beside the bed.'

'When was the dose taken?'

'It was the next day.'

'Did she take it herself?'

'No. She was very weak, and we thought she might spill it. Miss Mercer gave her a drink of water and the medicine. She helped give all Miss Caldie's medicine until she was on the mend.'

Holmes paused for a few moments of thought, then he continued. 'And what of Mr Caldie's recovery? Did he call a doctor or take any medicine?'

'I don't think so. He came to see his sister the next day, and I asked him how he was. He said that when he went home after being taken ill at dinner, he drank a large amount of brandy and was very sick indeed, and he thought it had carried everything away. Miss Mercer suggested he should try the medicine, but he smelt it and declared it to be vile stuff and would have none of it. He said brandy was the best medicine.'

'It does have medicinal uses,' I observed.

'Not in the quantities Mr Caldie consumes,' said Mrs McGillivray. 'But in this case, it might have saved him from something worse as it made him so sick.'

Holmes reflected on this information. 'This dinner, at which the Caldies and Miss Mercer were all present, do you know what was discussed?'

'I only heard a little when I served at table,' said the housekeeper. 'Something to do with a horse, I believe.'

'Have there been any similar incidents since then, regarding either Miss or Mr Caldie?'

'No, at least I know that Miss Caldie has been in her usual excellent health for the last four months. I can't speak for Mr Caldie. I have heard nothing to suggest he has been unwell.'

That was all the housekeeper was able to tell us, and she left to inform Miss Caldie that the interview was over before she returned to her duties.

Holmes stared at the bottle before he returned it to the paper bag and placed it in his pocket, careful to keep it upright. 'When two people sit down to dinner and eat the same thing and are both taken ill very soon afterwards, I think we can discount any cause other than what they have consumed,' he said. 'The cause may well have been bad fish, and the housekeeper ate only a small portion which might have been good, and therefore suffered no ill effects. But this bottle and its effects raise other suspicions, and I must subject the contents to tests before I arrive at any conclusions. I will not mention this to Miss Caldie until I have the results.'

At this moment, Miss Caldie and Miss Mercer returned to the drawing room.

'My interview with Mrs McGillivray may well be useful,' said Holmes. 'But I now have further work to do. I will report to you once more when it is completed.' Farewells were polite and perfunctory, and Miss Mercer saw us to the door without speaking.

'You appreciate why I was so interested in Mr McCaskie's receipt for silver polish?' asked Holmes, as we walked away.

I decided not to offer a guess, which might only have made me appear foolish. 'I'm afraid not.'

'Butlers often keep notes to assist them, a book of their most reliable formulations, and I hoped that Mr McCaskie had done so. Not only do I now have a proven receipt for silver polish, but I can also confirm that the butler did not write the label on the specimen of the great auk.'

'There was something you saw which surprised you when you read the entry on the great auk in the book of British birds,' I said.

'That is true, and I have some enquiries to make as a result.'

'I read the article twice, and nothing sprang to mind,' I said.

'It wasn't in the article,' said Holmes.

CHAPTER TWENTY-TWO

John Watson's memoirs sometimes allude to the chemistry experiments Holmes carried out in their shared rooms at 221b Baker Street. Holmes's Montague Street apartment, where he lived during his early years in London, was quite unsuitable for such an activity. Not only was it too small, but it was also horribly cluttered, principally with material of a highly combustible nature. I think he did occasionally mix a few chemicals there, but had he set up a bench of gas burners and attempted to condense the vapour of boiling liquids, the world might never have known of Sherlock Holmes the famous detective, and we would have been the poorer for it. It was, I think, the need for somewhere to create his own personal laboratory once his courses at Barts were complete that prompted him to seek more spacious accommodation.

Fortunately, the chemistry laboratory at Barts had everything we needed to subject the contents of Miss Caldie's medicine bottle to a series of tests for the most common poisons. Given the nature of the symptoms and the rapidity of their onset, we already had our suspicions, and so made our initial tests for the presence of arsenic. It was unsurprising when we obtained a strong reaction.

Arsenic is widely employed medicinally for a great many conditions, but always in a very dilute solution, *liquor arsenicalis*. In this case, it was clear that Miss Caldie's bottle of mixture had been contaminated by the addition of powdered white arsenic in potentially lethal amounts.

'Miss Caldie has had a fortunate escape,' said Holmes. 'Whoever added arsenic to this bottle was unaware that the powder does not dissolve easily in cold fluids. Most of it would have sunk to the bottom and left the residue which Mrs McGillivray observed. There was no direction on the label to shake the bottle before use, which again, was fortunate. The result was that there was a small but still harmful concentration in the first dose taken.'

'That is not the kind of error a chemist would make,' I said.

'It is not. I will of course ask Professor Russell to confirm my findings before we make our report, but I am sure he will agree. And the police must be informed. I consider this to be the second attempt on Miss Caldie's life,' he added.

I was mystified for a moment, then I exclaimed, 'You mean the fish supper was the first?'

'Yes, if it was the fish. The symptoms in that incident point strongly to the presence of arsenic. The dinner and now this cannot be put down to coincidence. At least, it would be safer not to do so.'

'But the first attempt involved both brother and sister,' I said. 'If two people are poisoned at the same meal, do we know if both were the intended victims, or just one? The medicine confirms that Miss Caldie was a target. Perhaps the poisoning of her brother was unintentional. Or the poisoner cared nothing as to whether he lived or died. Or there might have been a second attempt on his life we know nothing about.'

'Given his mode of life, that might be hard to establish,' said Holmes. 'If he was taken ill again at a later date, he might have put it down to overindulgence and thought no more of it. I doubt that we will have any samples to test.'

'But the two attempts we know about were only a day apart, at most, and that was several months ago. What has happened since then?'

'There are several possibilities,' said Holmes. 'A later attempt might have failed. Or the would-be poisoner might not have had the opportunity, or simply decided against proceeding any further. Either way, the potential danger suggests we need to alert the Caldies. The brother, since he is absent from his usual haunts, may be safe at present, but if he can be found he should be warned. Miss Caldie must be told without delay.'

We were able to secure an immediate interview with Miss Caldie, who listened very attentively to what Holmes had to say. 'Are you implying that the incident with the fish dinner last December might have been an attempt to poison both myself and my brother?' she asked, incredulously. 'But you have no evidence of that, and it would be impossible to obtain any now. I find it hard to imagine who might have wanted to do such a thing.'

'I might have agreed with you, had the incident been an isolated one,' said Holmes. 'But the poisoned medicine —'

'Yes, that is more concerning. And you really think it could not have been a chemist's error? That seems to me to be the most likely explanation.'

'It is only one of several. But please tell me, and think very carefully — since that day when you and your brother were taken ill after the fish dinner, and the following day, when you were made worse by the medicine, have there been any similar suspicions or incidents regarding food or drink, or medicine?'

Miss Caldie gave this as much thought as she thought necessary and then shook her head very emphatically. 'No, none.'

'Has your brother told you of anything of that nature that has occurred to him?'

'No.'

'Have the two of you dined together since then?'

'Yes, several times.'

Holmes was thoughtful. 'Who would benefit had the two of you succumbed to poison?'

'You mean financially? It was shortly after the death of our grandfather and we knew from what he had told us that we would inherit equal shares in the estate, although the amount had not yet been quantified. I suppose,' she added reluctantly, 'I ought to mention that grandfather disapproved of our mother's second marriage and arranged to leave her nothing. If either I or Alastair had predeceased the other without making wills, then the living sibling was to inherit all. If both, then the entire fortune would have gone to educational charities. I, of course, have made a will.'

'Has your brother made a will?'

'I don't know. I very much doubt it.'

'Who are your legatees?'

Miss Caldie bridled a little at such a direct question but replied, 'Principally the Caldie Society, but there are other smaller charitable bequests, as well as Miss Mercer, and a small sum to Mrs McGillivray.'

'When did you make your will?'

'As soon as my inheritance was confirmed. Although the estate had not been valued, my share was expected to be substantial, and it was the prudent thing to do. Up to that time my funds were extremely modest, and the Caldie Society was merely a dream. I set about making it a reality, although there is much to be done before it is anything more than just a name.'

'How does Miss Mercer benefit?'

Miss Caldie understood the implications of this question but refused to be drawn into comment. 'Miss Mercer has been a valuable partner in all my undertakings. I have left her a lump sum to invest, and she will be a salaried employee and principal manager of the Society.'

'That might have dangers for an unattached woman,' said Holmes.

'Only if she seeks an attachment. Miss Mercer considers marriage to confer no advantages upon women. She prefers her own protection to that of a man. The legacy would have ensured her continued independence.'

'You have not named your brother in your will?'

'He will receive some family portraits. They are of sentimental value only.'

'Did he express an opinion on this?'

'I do not discuss the finer details of my bequests with my brother. But he is well aware that I do not intend to share my fortune with him. He would just fritter it away. He seemed quite offended when I told him of the Caldie Society. He said that young ladies are becoming too serious for his liking and ladies ought not to be serious until they are at least forty.'

'You did not appoint your brother as an executor of your will?'

'Do I appear to you to be insane, Mr Holmes?'

'No, far from it. Who is your executor?'

'Miss Mercer. She is my *confidante*. I trust her absolutely.'

Holmes took some moments to consider this information.

'Is that all you require, Mr Holmes?' asked Miss Caldie impatiently. 'If so, kindly take your leave, as I have a great deal to do.'

'I have one more question. What was the subject of the discussion at dinner on the day you and your brother were taken ill?'

'What relevance can that possibly have?'

'None, I am sure, but I have learned, often to my bitter regret, never to omit a detail, however trivial.'

Miss Caldie shrugged. 'If you must know, Alastair announced his intention to purchase a racehorse. I thought it a foolish and expensive scheme and said so. He thought he could make a fortune from it. He even asked me if I was interested in sharing half the "investment", as he called it, with him. I told him no. In fact, I made it very clear to him that when my grandfather's bequest was ultimately apportioned between the two of us, our financial affairs should be kept entirely separate. His interests and mine are quite different, and there is nothing to be gained from combining our funds in any enterprise.'

'Did he purchase the racehorse?'

'No. He came to me about a week later and said he had been outbid but would look for another. In fact, he asked me if I had changed my mind about purchasing a share, but I told him very firmly not to bother me with his schemes again. He was so annoyingly persistent that I was obliged to be blunt with him on the subject. I made it perfectly clear that all my funds, both in my lifetime and after my death, were to be devoted to charitable objects.'

'How did he respond to this?'

'He looked insulted and rushed away. I don't think I saw him again for a month. Please don't ask me what he had been doing in that time. I did not enquire after him and would rather not know.'

At this moment there was knock at the front door.

'Are you expecting a visitor?' asked Holmes.

'I am not.' It would have been polite to leave at that juncture, had there been a prior appointment, but since there was not, Holmes dared to remain.

Soon afterwards, Miss Mercer appeared. 'Miss Caldie, there is a policeman at the door asking to see you.'

'Does he have news of my brother?'

'He didn't say. I don't believe so.'

'Very well, show him in.' Miss Mercer went to admit the visitor. Miss Caldie looked at us, and it was clear she was highly irritated by the intrusion. 'I suppose this is your doing,' she said, accusingly.

'If you mean, did we report to the police our finding that your medicine had been poisoned with arsenic, yes, it is.'

She sighed. 'Yes, forgive me. That was your duty, of course. I see that.'

'We will see ourselves out,' said Holmes. 'But if there is anything we can do, please do not hesitate to ask.'

Miss Caldie assented, but she was desperately unhappy.

CHAPTER TWENTY-THREE

On the following day, Holmes received a note from Sergeant Lestrade which resulted in a meeting in my rooms. Lestrade arrived in an unusually buoyant mood.

'Well, Mr Holmes, you have certainly created a bit of a stir. My inspector was very doubtful about it all, but after a word with Professor Russell — who speaks very highly of you, I ought to say — he did look into it, and we can only agree that someone must have tried to poison Miss Caldie. We're just not sure who. Or why. Miss Caldie and Miss Mercer both insisted it must have been a mistake by the chemist. Very strange ladies both of them, very fixed in their ideas.

'However, we have spoken to the chemist, and he showed us how the mixture was dispensed from a big bottle he made up himself. He keeps a large quantity on hand, since it is something that is prescribed very often for ladies of a nervous disposition.'

I tried to imagine Miss Caldie in that light but failed.

'He said he had filled several prescriptions from that same bottle before and since, without any complaint,' Lestrade continued. 'We made sure to have a sample tested, and it was perfectly innocent. The medicine bottles he uses are all thoroughly cleaned. We tested several and they too showed no sign of contamination. We are perfectly satisfied that there was no mistake by the chemist.'

'There remains, of course, the progress of the bottle from the shop to Miss Caldie's bedside,' said Holmes. 'Have you established the details of this journey and who might have had the opportunity to add the arsenic?'

'I have personally interviewed Miss Mercer,' said Lestrade. 'The bottle was wrapped and sealed by the chemist before it was handed to her. She brought it home and did not unwrap it until she was in Miss Caldie's bedroom, where she placed it on the nightstand. She uncorked the bottle and smelt it but re-corked it again without tasting it herself. She was intending to give the first dose immediately, but Miss Caldie, exhausted from the powerful symptoms she had suffered, was enjoying the first peaceful sleep she had had for some time and Miss Mercer decided not to disturb her.'

'Who else was in the house at the time?'

'Only Mrs McGillivray. She says she did look in on Miss Caldie from time to time, but she denies touching the bottle.'

'Were there any visitors?'

'Two ladies who were interested in Miss Caldie's charities, but neither were allowed to enter the room.'

'Did Miss Mercer mention Mr Caldie arriving to see his sister the day after their meal?'

'She did. She enquired after his health, and he said he was much improved. He asked to see his sister and she said he was to be very quiet as she was asleep, but she admitted him to the room. She offered him some of the medicine, and he also smelt it but said it was horrid and he preferred brandy. Miss Mercer re-corked the bottle.'

'Did Mr Caldie actually handle the bottle?'

'No, he did not touch it. She merely passed it under his nose. Neither of them added anything to it.'

'And what of Mrs McGillivray?'

'She was in the kitchen making tea, and I do not think she entered Miss Caldie's bedroom.'

'How long did Mr Caldie remain?'

'Not very long. Miss Mercer invited him to take tea in the drawing room. He declined and went home.'

'When was the first dose actually given?'

'About midday, when Miss Caldie awoke saying she felt a little better. She does not like to take medicines and accepted only part of a teaspoonful. The symptoms began again not long afterwards. She refused to take any more.'

'According to these statements, for a number of hours the bottle of medicine stood on the nightstand, the cork having already been disturbed, beside a sleeping woman,' said Holmes.

'It did,' said Lestrade.

'Yet,' said Holmes, 'at some point, and by some human agency, the medicine was contaminated with poison, in such quantity that Miss Caldie was extremely fortunate to survive.'

'Yes, that is the difficulty,' admitted Lestrade. 'Do you have any observations, Mr Holmes?'

'Only that at least one person you have interviewed is not telling you the whole truth,' said Holmes, calmly.

Lestrade's mood darkened, as he must have contemplated revisiting his earlier efforts. 'And then, of course, we had to consider the indisposition of both brother and sister, the one supposed to have been caused by bad fish. I have spoken to Mr Caldie's manservant Mr Duncan, who purchased the fish, and Mrs McGillivray, who cooked it. Neither suspected anything wrong. Mr Duncan told me that on the day of the fish dinner, his master came home earlier than expected in a cab saying he felt very unwell, called for a bottle of brandy, and went to bed. After a number of bilious bouts his condition improved, but he was not able to stir from his bed until much later the next day, when he went to see if his sister was better. He did not call a doctor. There's not much we can do about that, and my inspector is tempted to believe that it was the fish.

Perhaps the individual who poisoned the medicine decided to take advantage of Miss Caldie's state of health, hoping her death might be attributed to something she had eaten. But there is no arsenic in the apartment, and no record of any member of the family or their servants having bought any. Mr Duncan is adamant that neither he nor Mr Caldie have ever purchased arsenic, although he admits that the brother's rooms are often crowded with visitors of colourful reputation.'

I could see that Holmes was not pleased with this dismissal of his theory, but he made no protest.

'But you will be pleased to know,' Lestrade went on, rather more cheerily, 'that we have made a significant advance in the case of Mr Smith. I am greatly indebted to you for the enquiries you made along the route taken by Smith on his way to the place where he was murdered. The trinket box, a very delicate little item, we think might have been a gift for his lady friend in New Zealand. The assistant who sold it recalls only that Smith was unaccompanied when he was in the shop. We have also interviewed the assistant at the shop selling pipe tobacco, and other locations nearby, where the man following him might have been seen passing by. This man does not appear to have entered any shops. The best description we have is that he was aged between twenty-five and forty, of respectable appearance, clean-shaven, and wore a round hat. I think you will agree that this man, whoever he was, could not have been any of the gentlemen from the museum who were present at the disturbance over the great auk.'

'I agree,' said Holmes.

'We then re-interviewed Mr Smith's associate, Mr Selby, and also spoke to the owners of the shop on the floor below the office of the *Natural History Review*, and they have an interesting tale to tell. They recalled the last day on which Mr Smith met with Mr Selby and said that they overheard a heated exchange between the two men. They were unable to make out exactly what was being said, but it was very clear to them that tempers were raised. Shortly after Mr Smith left, Mr Selby went out.

'We asked Mr Selby about this, and his account is that Smith was overwrought about recent events and expressed himself forcefully. Selby says he simply tried to calm him down and claims that there was no disagreement. He admits that he left the office soon afterwards but denies following Smith or harming him in any way. He said he went home to tell his wife that he was to be made editor of the journal at an improved salary, and that they would be able to rent the Smiths' villa. Naturally, Mrs Selby supports his story. A wife usually does unless she has reasons not to. But it has to be said that Selby does match the description of the man seen following Smith.'

'You suspect him of the crime?' exclaimed Holmes in astonishment.

'The way I see it,' said Lestrade, 'is that we only have his account of the conversation with Smith, and a wife's evidence as to her husband's movements are worthless in court.'

'But why would Selby wish to do away with Smith?' Holmes protested.

'Well, remember, only Selby and the dead man know what they discussed that day. My theory is that Smith, wanting to settle his affairs before he left for New Zealand, had found something regarding the management of the *Review* that displeased him and decided to terminate Mr Selby's employment. That is what the argument was about, and why the people downstairs heard raised voices. Mr Selby, with a growing family to support, and facing a loss of income and possibly a blot on his career, decided to take drastic action. We have taken him into custody, and hope that questioning will uncover the truth.'

'I believe that the murderer stole several items from Smith's body,' said Holmes. 'The watch, the pocketbook, which has most probably been emptied of anything of value and thrown away, the trinket box, and a recently purchased pouch of tobacco. But Mr Selby did not smoke tobacco. If he had done so, I think the odour of it would have been apparent in his office, but I did not detect any. I saw none of the usual accoutrements of a smoker.'

'A gift for a relative, perhaps?' suggested Lestrade.

'That should be easy to discover, given that I have supplied you with the details of the brand purchased. And then there is the trinket box. Quite a distinctive little item. Has Mrs Selby recently acquired one? Heaven forfend there is another lady who has a place in Mr Selby's affections. Have you enquired at the pawnshops?'

Lestrade was becoming a little irritated by Holmes's objections. 'I can see you think we are on the wrong track, Mr Holmes, but this is the best theory we have at present. At least we may both be confident that Smith was not killed over a disagreement about a stuffed bird.'

'With that, at least, I can agree,' said Holmes. 'The great auk was not the cause of his death, merely the means of drawing me into the case, and thereafter was merely an interested spectator.'

CHAPTER TWENTY-FOUR

Holmes had been hoping to interview Mrs Smith once more. He had written to Mrs Roper, enquiring after her sister's health and asking to make an appointment in order to advise her regarding the current state of the investigation. He received the following reply.

Dear Mr Holmes,

I am sorry to say my poor sister is not improved, and I feel that any recovery she is able to make will be very slow. She will, I fear, never be the robust creature she once was. I am dealing with all her affairs at present, as she is very distressed at some recent developments concerning her financial position. If you are agreeable, I will meet with you at Park Villa tomorrow at 10 o'clock and will convey any news you bring to my sister when she is able to appreciate it.

J. Roper (Mrs)

We met Mrs Roper in the same gloomy drawing room, although with the absence of Mrs Smith some light was allowed to enter, so it was possible to examine papers. There were a few simple refreshments, brought by the same strong-faced maid.

Mrs Roper had a bundle of documents, which we were permitted to see.

'My sister is quite incapable of dealing with her financial affairs and asked me and her solicitor to take on that task,' she said. 'She was particularly concerned about her late husband's collection of fossils and his dealings with the bank. I am sorry to say the shock to her has been considerable. Over the years

Robert kept a very detailed record of all his acquisitions, noting when they were purchased, how much they cost and the value he thought they would fetch if sold. It all appeared very promising.' She handed us a set of schedules written up in spiky black-inked lettering. 'As you see, he was quite meticulous. But the value was only what he believed they were worth; he never sought any advice on the matter. They have now been officially valued and put up for auction, but it appears that they have not appreciated as much as he had hoped. The expert who examined them has placed a much lower estimate. We do not know what they might fetch, and there will also be the auctioneer's fees to pay, but they should produce something. We were already aware that Robert had been overdrawing his bank accounts in order to purchase these items, and the banks require settlement. However —' she rubbed her eyes, pinching the bridge of her nose with a pained grimace, before continuing — 'I am sorry to say that other creditors have recently come forward with records of loans which have come due for repayment, and the situation is far worse than we had feared. All in all, after the debts have been paid there will be almost nothing left.'

'You mentioned that Mrs Smith has some income of her own,' said Holmes. 'And there is the lease, of course.'

'Her income is not great and as to the lease, that is a sore point,' said Mrs Roper. 'You may have wondered why Robert left the lease to Charles, when he was living in New Zealand and unlikely ever to make his home here again.'

'Did Professor Smith know that his son intended to settle there when he made the will?' asked Holmes.

'He did not. Robert made the will when Charles reached his majority, and at the time the visit to New Zealand was anticipated only to be about six months or a year at most. But after a year Charles wrote to his parents saying he wished to stay there. Phoebe told Robert that that being the case, she ought to be named as inheritor of the lease. Robert was not willing to do this, for if she remarried the lease would be under the control of her new husband, and things might become very complicated indeed. Phoebe promised him she would never remarry and would make sure that Charles inherited the lease on her death. In any case, she said her son would always have a home here if he should require it. Eventually, after a great deal of debate, Robert agreed to her request and went to a solicitor about it. When he returned, he told Phoebe that all had been dealt with as she wished. The will was lodged with the solicitor. My late husband was named as executor. I myself thought no more of it, and neither, I think, did Phoebe.'

Mrs Roper looked grim as she continued. 'On Robert's death, Phoebe found she had not been told the truth. The lease was inherited by her son, and she had only the lifetime right to live in the house unless she remarried. Phoebe was very upset. Not that the terms of the will made any difference to her, but she knew that her husband had lied because he did not trust her.'

'Has your sister ever intimated to you that she wished to remarry?' asked Holmes.

'No, not at all. And I don't believe she has received any gentlemen callers. At least not of that kind.'

'Have there been any gentlemen callers at all? I mean in the last few months, both before Professor Smith's death and afterwards.'

'Mr Selby used to visit sometimes after Charles came home, to talk business with him. And then of course Dr Scales used to come in a professional way. Both are respectable married gentlemen. Then — well — I know I said before about the coal man Mr Hepden, and the maid, Jenny.'

'You said that he was talking to her. He surely does not enter the house?' exclaimed Holmes.

'Not on his rounds, no, but on Sunday afternoons after church, he comes to the kitchen and sits down there and has his tea. It seems they are courting. I didn't approve, and I told Phoebe so. Had that been the case with my maid, she would have been dismissed at once, but it is up to Phoebe whom she allows in her house. And Mr Charles was always letting his mother do what she wished if it contented her.'

'How long have they been courting?'

'Since last Christmas, I think, although they kept it very quiet at first. I only heard about it after Robert died.'

'Did Professor Smith not object to the coal man's visits?'

'He might have done, if he had known about them, but he always said the singing in church made his head go round, and when he came back, he went and sat in his study, or took a nap.'

Holmes looked thoughtful, and I was relieved when he abandoned the subject of the coal man's romantic inclinations. 'Did Professor Smith's will make any provisions for his estate in the event of his son dying without issue before his mother, as has been the sad case here?'

'No, none, so Phoebe has inherited the property now. But I don't think she can hope to maintain it. I have suggested she sells or rents it out and comes to live with me. She is still considering that offer.'

'She has no-one else to assist her?'

'No, although she has received a large number of letters of condolence. The usual offers of help which never seem to amount to much. They continue to arrive, and I am still dealing with them.'

'Nothing from Professor Owen, I take it?' said Holmes.

'Not that I can recall,' said Mrs Roper.

'Might I see any letters that came from the museum or professional acquaintances? Or correspondence for Mr Smith himself? Did he retain his letters?'

'I will see what I can find,' said Mrs Roper.

While she was absent from the room, I turned to Holmes. 'Surely,' I said, 'Mrs Smith was in no worse a position, despite the misunderstanding about the will, after her husband's death? He told her she would always have a roof over her head and that was what he granted her.'

'That is true, unless she wished to remarry, of which we have no suggestion,' said Holmes. 'Unless…' He stopped. 'There are a hundred little facts in this case which ought to fit together to make a complete picture, but I cannot connect them as yet.'

Mrs Roper returned with the letters. 'There was a letter from the University and some from Robert's students.' She passed them to us, and Holmes glanced through them without comment.

'Oh, and this is a letter of condolence from Mr Selby to my sister, and this one — I am not sure why I still have this — it is from the museum to Charles regarding his application to attend the unveiling. I can't help wondering — if he had never gone, or if he had never made such a fuss, would he still be alive now?'

Both these letters were brief. Selby's expressed shock and sympathy at the terrible news and suggested that if Mrs Smith should require anything, she had only to ask. The other was a formal acceptance of the application, mentioning that a ticket was enclosed. It was signed by Professor Beare. Only one of these letters engaged Holmes's strong attention. He showed it to me. 'We have seen this handwriting before,' he said, and I had to agree. It was the handwriting on the label of the great auk.

'What does it mean?' I asked.

'A confrontation with someone who has a great deal to hide,' said Holmes. 'But he will not admit it readily unless I can present him with undeniable proof, which is not yet in my possession. I mean to obtain it.'

CHAPTER TWENTY-FIVE

I was under strict instructions to say nothing about our discovery until Holmes had found the proof he needed. In the meantime, my studies were calling. I was at home, allowing myself to sink into the welcome distraction of my medical books, when there was a knock at my door. I knew it was not Holmes, since he tended to give a sharp rap of the cane followed by an immediate entry. My landlady peered in and said that a Mr Duncan had come asking to see me. I had not expected to hear from him again, and my expression of astonishment must have suggested to her that I had no idea who the caller was. 'He has one of your cards,' she added.

'Show him up,' I said, quickly tidying my papers. I waited, hoping that Alastair Caldie's manservant had finally learned where his master was.

Mr Duncan appeared at the door, looking jaded and unhappy. I invited him in.

'May I help you?' I asked, offering him a chair. 'Do you have news of Mr Caldie?'

He sat down rather heavily, although he was not a heavy man. I had not studied him before, but I realised that while he might be regarded as an aged retainer, he was probably under fifty. Sparse strands of grey hair were all he had to cover his pate, and I imagined he had given much of his health and energy in the service of the Caldie family.

'It's been a bad time,' he said. 'No, Mr Caldie has not returned, and I have heard nothing from him, not a letter or a message of any kind. The police have been round asking after him; I don't know what that is about. I know Miss Caldie is trying to find him, and she has my sympathy, but I don't know how I can go on. There are some men from the Wheatsheaf, and they keep coming and asking if he is home, and I don't like them at all. Then there is the butcher and the wine merchant and the tailor. All are owed money. They have been sending letters, and soon enough I know there will be men coming to the door with demands. There is no money left even for necessities. Mr Caldie borrowed my little bit of savings before he left, I haven't been paid my wages in weeks, and just this morning the landlord came saying he was owed rent and was going to go to law unless it was paid. What am I to do?'

'Miss Caldie has promised his most pressing creditors that if she can find her brother, she will arrange for them to be paid,' I said. 'But of course, she may not know about all his debts. In fact, when I saw her last, I don't think she knew about the rent and the other things, although she may have suspected that was the position.'

'Didn't he inherit all that money from his grandfather?' asked Duncan plaintively.

'I believe it has all gone,' I said. 'I think he ran up debts in anticipation of the inheritance. But he does have some property his sister can arrange to be sold once he is found.'

Mr Duncan looked so miserable I wondered if there was anything I could do to help him. 'Perhaps,' I said, 'if you could think very hard, you might remember something that could help find Mr Caldie. It might be something very small, so trivial you would not think it important, but it could prove to be the key.'

He did not appear to be encouraged by this; rather, he gave me a haunted look. 'There is something,' he said. 'But I am not sure if I dare say it.'

I waited for him to go on, but he faltered and lapsed into silence. 'Come with me,' I said. 'My friend Mr Holmes — he is the gentleman who called on Miss Caldie with me not long ago — is a very clever man, and you should talk to him.'

Mr Duncan agreed to accompany me, although when he stood, he wavered so much on his legs that I feared he was about to faint. I thought he might not have eaten recently, and I arranged for him to have hot tea and bread and butter before we departed, which seemed to strengthen him a little.

Fortunately, I found Holmes at Barts, in the chemistry laboratory, watching over one of his more esoteric experiments. He sat Mr Duncan down, adjusted the gas burners to a less dangerous level, and gave our visitor his full attention.

'I haven't heard from Mr Caldie, and I can't help feeling he doesn't want to be found by anyone,' said Duncan. 'Not the creditors, nor the police I am sure, and not even his own sister.'

'How interesting,' mused Holmes. 'And,' he continued in a more sympathetic tone, 'he must have left you in such a difficult position, that you scarcely know what to do.'

'He has. If it goes on much longer, I won't have a roof over my head, and all his possessions and my few things will be out in the street.'

'That is a very thoughtless way to behave,' said Holmes. 'I understand you have given exemplary service for some years.'

'I have, and under some very trying circumstances. Sometimes I have to turn aside and not look at all that goes on.'

Holmes paced up and down, appearing to be giving the manservant's difficulty the most profound thought. 'Has Mr Caldie let slip anything to say where he has gone?'

'No, although I know Miss Caldie has all the addresses where he might be. But I think — even if he does come back, I have to say to him, I must find another place.'

'That would be advisable. I am sure that Miss Caldie, who is well acquainted with her brother's failings, would give you a glowing character which would secure you a better position,' said Holmes. 'Especially when you have revealed what it is you are about to tell me.'

Mr Duncan looked surprised, then abashed. 'I don't know if I can. Or if I ought.'

Holmes drew up a stool and perched his long frame on it, his body hunched forward, gazing very earnestly at the unhappy servant. 'You are tormented by what you know, what you have not yet revealed. You have acted throughout with the highest motives, from loyalty to your master, following his instructions to the letter, but now his behaviour has led you to the very brink of desperation and destitution. No-one would blame you now for telling me all.'

'Thank you, sir,' said Duncan gratefully. 'I wish everyone would think like you. But I fear there has been a crime committed and I have been drawn into it.'

'When a servant acts under the direction of his master, the law does not hold him responsible,' said Holmes. 'It is the master who must bear the blame. But before we discuss where Mr Caldie might be, let us talk about something else. Last December, when he dined at his sister's. I think that is what is troubling you, is it not?'

'Yes, sir,' Duncan admitted.

'You purchased the fish, did you not? What can you tell me about that?'

'Well, sir, I ordered the fish as Mr Caldie directed and the fishmonger's boy delivered it. But Mr Caldie came back home earlier than expected. He said he had had a dinner which was very dull, and the conversation was even duller. He sent me out to get brandy to wash away the taste. And he spent the rest of the night drinking until he fell asleep. The next morning, he said that if anyone was to ask about him, I was to tell them he had eaten some bad fish at his sister's house and was very ill and had to stay in bed. That was the story, and I was never to say anything else. Even if a doctor came and asked, or the police, he said I had to tell them the same thing.'

'But Mr Caldie was not ill that night, was he?' said Holmes. 'He had none of the symptoms you would expect from food poisoning?'

'No, none. I did wonder why he told me to tell an untruth. I thought at first that he had taken too much to drink and didn't like to admit to being unwell. But then, later, I started thinking. And when he ran away, I thought some more.'

'I am greatly indebted to you,' said Holmes. 'I have suspected for some time that Mr Caldie tried to poison his sister at that meal, and only feigned illness to suggest that the fish, which only the two of them had eaten, was at fault. I am sure if we were to question the housekeeper, Mrs McGillivray, she might recall him entering the kitchen while Miss Caldie's tisane was steeping and distracting her. It was the one thing served that evening that only Miss Caldie partook of.'

'But where did he get the arsenic?' I asked. 'Mr Duncan, you didn't buy any?'

'Oh no,' said Duncan, rather shocked at the suggestion. 'I don't think it has any place in a gentleman's home. If Mr Caldie had some, I suppose it would have been among his private possessions, which I was not to touch. I always supposed he kept stimulants there. It was not for me to comment.'

'Last December, Mr and Miss Caldie went to Scotland to oversee the sale of the manor house and its contents,' said Holmes. 'Sir Andrew's workshop where he used to prepare his specimens would have been amply supplied with arsenic, which taxidermists use in the preservation of skins.' He turned to Duncan. 'I attach no blame of any kind to you. You did as you were commanded by your master, and it took considerable courage to come forward. Whether it will be possible to bring the accusation home to Mr Caldie, I cannot say. But you must now go to the police and tell them what you know. If you explain that on reflection you do not think Mr Caldie told you the truth, but pressed you into believing his account, I doubt that there will be any consequences.'

'Do you think so?' said Duncan, hopefully.

'I know a friendly sergeant of police and will accompany you to a meeting with him, at which I will sing your praises,' promised Holmes.

Mr Duncan looked more cheerful.

'But why did Caldie try to poison his sister?' I asked.

'For money,' said Holmes. 'Her half of the inheritance. Recall that the fish dinner took place quite soon after the death of their grandfather, who had told them he would share his fortune with them. They would have expected a substantial settlement, but it had not yet been quantified. Caldie must have assumed that he would automatically benefit from his sister's death. He had no idea that she had immediately taken steps to protect her fortune by making a will. Lazy persons like Caldie can never quite anticipate the efficiency of others, even when they already know them to be efficient.'

'I hope he can be located,' I said.

Mr Duncan gave a polite cough, then extracted a paper from his pocket. 'I — er — found this recently,' he said. 'It may be of some help. It — um — fell from between the pages of the *Sporting Gazette* as I was tiding some papers.'

Holmes examined the document, which was an advertising leaflet for a Scottish guest house. 'What a marvel you are!' he exclaimed.

Holmes was as good as his word, accompanying the nervous manservant to tell his tale to the police. Duncan was reassured that since he had been acting under the instructions of his master, no blame would be attached to him for concealing the truth.

The one thing we lacked was how the second poisoning had been achieved. Holmes had no doubt that it was Caldie who had made the second attempt but had yet to establish how it had been done. 'I suggest to you, Lestrade,' he told the sergeant, 'that the person you need to interview is Miss Mercer.'

'You think she was in collusion with Caldie?' exclaimed Lestrade. 'Very well, if that is the case, I will get the truth from her.'

'I do not think they were in collusion,' said Holmes, 'neither do I think she knows of his villainy and is protecting him. There is one way I believe he might have gained access to the medicine bottle undetected. Now that we know of the first attempt, I think she might at last be persuaded to speak.'

'I will see her myself,' said Lestrade. 'But if it was Caldie, why did he never make another attempt?'

'In the conversation with his sister a week later, he discovered that she had already made a will and one from which he would not benefit.'

'Ah,' said Lestrade. 'Money.'

'It usually is,' said Holmes. 'How I long to discover crimes committed from high principles and noble motives. But they are rarities, I fear.'

We were later informed that Miss Mercer had with extreme reluctance revealed the whole truth of Alastair Caldie's visit to his sister on the day after the fish dinner. He had not, as she had initially claimed, departed after declining tea. He had accepted the offer and they had waited for the tea to be brought into the drawing room. There he had unexpectedly addressed Miss Mercer in terms which she refused to repeat, since she found them vulgar and insulting. She had asked him to leave immediately, but he had persisted with attentions which had disgusted her. Mrs McGillivray was still in the kitchen, and Miss Mercer had been obliged to run in that direction for safety. Caldie followed her but did not enter the kitchen. He merely smiled and said he would see himself out. Naturally Miss Mercer did not see him to the door, but as her pursuer turned to leave, she entered the kitchen and made conversation with the housekeeper, whom she thought suspected nothing of what had just transpired. When the tea was brought, she found to her relief that Mr Caldie had departed.

'And that was when it was done,' said Holmes. 'He had already seen the bottle, he knew the cork had been disturbed, and he had come prepared with a packet of arsenic, looking for an opportunity to administer it unobserved. Miss Caldie was asleep; Miss Mercer and the housekeeper were in the kitchen. It was the work of moments to do what he did, and then he left. So soon after the fish dinner, he thought his sister's death would simply be put down to a relapse.'

The revelation that we suspected Alastair Caldie had twice attempted to poison his own sister for her fortune was a terrible blow to that lady. When we explained it to Miss Caldie, I saw her recoil with shock, just for a moment, then make a determined effort to control her emotions. She questioned us in detail, looking for some circumstance that might harm our theory and allow her to reject it. Eventually she was obliged to agree with us. She had, I think, been fond of her undisciplined brother, and it was hard for her to accept that he was capable of such treachery. She had, over the years, forgiven him a great deal, but there are some things that cannot be forgiven.

'And I see it all now; he never had any intention of purchasing a racehorse,' she said. 'It was just a scheme to extract money from me.' She thanked us for the paper with the address of the guest house in Scotland. 'I am not sure if he has ever been there, but it is in an area he has been known to visit. I will advise my solicitor that he might be there and hope to secure him. And I am afraid the police must be involved, too.'

'The police have already been advised,' said Holmes. 'I have heard only today that he has been found and placed under arrest.'

Holmes was entirely satisfied that Alastair Caldie had twice attempted to murder his sister, but his opinion was not to carry any weight. We were later to learn that Caldie had been questioned at length regarding the suspected poisonings, but no charges were brought, as it was thought that the case against him would probably not succeed in court. No-one had seen him administer poison, no trace of arsenic was found in his possession and there was no evidence that he had ever had any. Miss Caldie's doctor, who had diagnosed food poisoning from bad fish, was not about to admit a mistake and made suggestions implying that the chemist's young assistant had been at fault regarding the medicine.

Miss Caldie did not leave her brother to the tender mercies of Mr Gough and Mr French. She had given them her solemn promise to attend to those debts, and it would have been contrary to her character to renege upon it.

While her brother remained in Scotland, Miss Caldie's solicitor made the arrangements to transfer to her a parcel of land which she duly sold, and Mr Gough received what he was owed. She also provided a good character for Mr Duncan, who was able to find a far pleasanter position than the one he had previously occupied.

There was to be no forgiveness for Alastair Caldie. He received a formal letter in which his sister, without any reference to his attack upon her person, stated that this was the first and last time she would arrange for settlement of his debts. She had no wish to see him again, and henceforward he would be a stranger to her. The cold implacability of this declaration left no room for doubt.

Caldie returned to a London in which he was no longer welcome, a home whose doors were locked against him, a forced sale of his personal property, and creditors' demands which sent him into bankruptcy. Soon afterwards, he disappeared once more. This time, no-one went looking for him.

CHAPTER TWENTY-SIX

'Holmes,' I said, not long afterwards. 'Have you had any news from Lestrade about Mr Selby? Has he been charged with the murder of Charles Smith?'

We were in the chemistry laboratory where Holmes, his fingertips embellished with scraps of sticking plaster, was devoting close attention to devising an improved method of testing for the presence of blood which would be effective on samples of any age. I was merely an interested observer and the occasional extra pair of hands, although I could see from his expression that the work had reached an impasse he could not breach.

'The police would have been most unwise to charge Selby, since their case is based on speculation without a fact to support it,' he said drily. 'But I have been told that the assistant at the tobacconists who saw the man following Smith has been asked if Selby is the man, and he was adamant that he was not. He was sure he saw a younger man. Lestrade is still not convinced, as he believes the strain of recent events have made Selby look older than his years. He has been obliged to release Selby without charge but is still keeping an eye on him.'

'You have said that the most common motive for murder is money.'

'That is true. Then there is love, in both its highest and lowest forms. Revenge for a slight. To prevent the witness of a crime giving evidence. The other causes are the senseless vulgar brawl, or a seizure of madness, which are of no interest.'

'Do you still think money was involved in the murder of Charles Smith? Because I have been giving this some thought, and an idea has struck me.'

There was a brief silence during which Holmes added some drops of fluid from a test tube to a vessel of clear liquid. There was no apparent result and he sighed in disappointment, returned the test tube to its rack, and turned his attention to me. 'Kindly enlighten me,' he said.

'I know you don't usually give any weight to my theories,' I said.

'This is true, but it would be unfriendly to ignore them without hearing them first. And they do occasionally have some merit.'

I dared to continue. 'You remember Mrs Bailey's Aunt Jane? She talked about a hussy making eyes at a man. She was quite disgusted by it. I suppose I assumed that she meant the Smiths' maid and her assignations with the coal man, which Mrs Roper so objected to. But maybe she was referring to something else. The maid — I mean, I am not a judge of such things, but I think she has a good face and figure, and a man might think her interesting. And not long ago, Mr Charles Smith came back to London to stay with his mother. If the maid had ambitions and hoped to make a catch above her station, she could have been "making eyes", as Aunt Jane put it, at Smith. Whether he thought anything of it, we shall never know. But supposing the coal man grew jealous? Maybe he thought he might be supplanted by a better placed rival? It is only a theory, of course,' I added defensively, 'and Aunt Jane, if her hearing and eyes are not as sharp as they once were, and if she has little to occupy her, might be imagining a scandal where none exists.'

To my surprise, Holmes did not dismiss my theory immediately but appeared to be giving it some thought, although he did not tell me his conclusions.

Any hopes that giving further time for a reaction to take place in his experiment had passed, and the trial had to be abandoned, although he remained determined that one day he would meet with success.

'And now,' he said, consulting his watch, 'we must return to the British Museum. I have secured another interview with the distinguished ornithologists which I think will greatly advance my enquiries.'

'Gentlemen,' said Holmes solemnly, as we faced Professor Beare and Dr Woodley across the desk once more. 'You asked me to try and establish the authenticity of the great auk specimen bequeathed by Sir Andrew Caldie. You required me to do so without either subjecting it to a potentially damaging examination or making enquiries in St Kilda, where it is supposed to have been collected. These restrictions have made my task extremely difficult, in fact almost impossible. But I have made a small advance, and while I am unable to offer you any certainty, I do have evidence which is suggestive.'

Our listeners waited with anticipation.

'I must begin with an apology, a humble admission that I was not sufficiently thorough in my research,' Holmes continued. 'I have been somewhat remiss in not fully investigating the history of the great auk as a species — *Pinguinus impennis*, as it is known to science, and as it is labelled in the museum, but it was not always so. Sir Andrew was not an ornithologist but an amateur collector. His main interest was the birds of South America; in fact, he possessed only one volume on the subject of British birds, an old edition by Bewick. This does include a description of the great auk, but in that book the caption reads, "*Alca impennis*". Could this have been an error? No, it was not. I made further enquiries and discovered that when the bird was originally allocated a genus, it was thought to be more closely related to the razorbill, *Alca torda*, but in recent years that opinion has changed; therefore, the name has been amended. I allowed myself to be misled by Sir Andrew's handwriting, which has its own very considerable inconstancies. When he referred to the specimen which he purchased from the unnamed visitor in 1855, he named it, as I thought, "Alca t", but of course I now realise it could as well have been "Alca i". The remainder of the word is not legible. I think it therefore very probable that Sir Andrew is referring to the item which he later bequeathed to the museum and which you now have in your collection, and it is indeed as you hoped and believed a complete skin of the great auk, albeit in very decayed condition.'

'Well, that is good news,' said Professor Beare, with an exhalation of relief. 'Is it possible, do you think, since the skin had been so poorly preserved, to make any progress as to the date it was collected?'

'To do so it would be necessary to discover the identity of the man who brought the skin to Sir Andrew,' said Holmes. 'Only he might be able to advise me. Might I be permitted to examine the label once more?'

'Do you think that will help us?' asked Beare. 'To discover who might have written it after so many years — and as you have said, it was most probably Sir Andrew's manservant.'

'Nevertheless,' said Holmes, 'please indulge me.'

Beare unlocked his desk drawer, withdrew the envelope and passed the label to Holmes, who studied it with his magnifying glass. 'This blot of ink which has been smeared might, I think, conceal something,' said Holmes. 'A marking, which, if I am correct, the writer is anxious should not be seen. My glass is not powerful enough to properly examine it, however. I had hoped to take it to Barts and place it under a more powerful lens, but you have already told me that I cannot remove the label from your possession.'

'That is still the case,' said Dr Woodley, and Professor Beare nodded agreement.

'Fear not,' said Holmes, with a smile. 'I have found another way. If the label cannot be brought to the microscope, then the microscope must be brought to the label.' Before either gentleman could comment on this, Holmes delved into his pocket and produced a brass implement, rather like a telescope, which he extended in a similar manner. 'I took the liberty of borrowing this from a fellow student,' he said. 'A field microscope, not as powerful as the larger ones we have in the laboratories, but I think it will serve my purpose. Stamford, bring the lamp closer.'

I moved the lamp to cast sufficient illumination, and Holmes produced a set of forceps to lift the label and place it under the lens. Beare and Woodley stared at him apprehensively, and Holmes could not resist a smile. 'I should mention, gentlemen, that I already know the identity of the author of this label, and can provide the proof, but this examination will confirm what I already know.'

'What are you looking for?' demanded Professor Beare.

'A signature,' said Holmes. 'The author appended his initials, which will be revealed by a closer inspection.' He spent some moments adjusting the little device, then at last gave an exclamation of triumph. 'Aha! Yes, here it is, clear as day if one knows what to look for.'

'Does it add anything to our knowledge of when the specimen was collected?' asked Beare.

'It does not,' said Holmes. 'Only one man can tell us that.'

'And you know who that man is?'

'I do.'

'Do you mean to interview him?'

'That is the only way I can achieve what I was requested to do.'

'Then please enlighten us,' said Beare.

'Not yet,' said Holmes, 'and certainly not before the interview has taken place. The man who collected the specimen has secrets to keep, and the affair must proceed with some delicacy.'

He folded away the little microscope and replaced it in his pocket. 'And now I must take my leave of you. I think before I depart, I will take the opportunity of a further tour of the bird collection here, which has proved to be so unexpectedly fascinating.'

We said our farewells, and I followed Holmes to the long gallery.

'What are you looking for?' I asked. 'We know it was Professor Beare who wrote the label.'

Holmes merely smiled. We waited awhile, and after a few minutes Dr Woodley approached us with an apologetic air. 'Gentlemen,' he said, 'I think it is time I spoke to you more candidly.'

CHAPTER TWENTY-SEVEN

Following our meeting, Professor Beare had gone to address a class of students and we were able to accompany Dr Woodley to the office to speak privately.

'How did you know about the authorship of the label?' he asked.

'I was recently shown a letter signed by Professor Beare, and I recognised the hand,' said Holmes. He produced that item of evidence from his pocket. Woodley recognised it and his face paled, but he did not reply. 'Even after the interval of so many years, the match was quite obvious,' Holmes continued relentlessly. 'The professor's eyesight has been failing, has it not? The signature was his, but the body of the letter was written by you. And my suspicions were confirmed when I saw that you had signed the label. The marking under the ink blot was not, as it might have appeared, a mere scribble, but your initials, V.W.W. The blot and smear appear under higher magnification to be more recent than the signature underneath. I believe that was your attempt to conceal your involvement. I am sure Professor Beare knows nothing of it.'

'Mr Holmes, I beg of you!' exclaimed Woodley with a sudden burst of emotion. 'You have discovered my secret, or at least a part of it. Please, I appeal to you as a man of honour not to reveal it, especially to Professor Beare, whose disapproval would be unendurable to me! Yes, it was I who sold the specimen to Sir Andrew Caldie all those years ago. And it was a genuine great auk, though much decayed. You do not know how relieved I was when Professor Beare did not recognise my hand on the label. And I admit it was I who tried to conceal the initials so they could not be read, or so I hoped. What Sir Andrew did with the skin, I cannot know, as I did not assist him. But when he bequeathed it to the museum, I recognised it at once. And I did write my initials and the date and place on a dried portion of the interior, so if it had been probed my secret could well have been revealed. But you must believe me, I have committed no crime, no fraud.'

'According to Sir Andrew's diaries, he obtained the specimen from a man who said he had been given it by his grandmother in St Kilda,' said Holmes. 'Was that true?'

'Not — precisely,' said Woodley, heavily.

Holmes's expression was grim as stone. 'If not precisely, then not at all,' he said. 'If I am to believe that no crime or scientific fraud has taken place, I need to know all the circumstances. Once I am satisfied of that, I will keep your secret.'

Woodley struggled for a moment, then he nodded and uttered a ragged sigh. 'I swear upon all that is holy I will tell you the truth.'

'Kindly proceed,' said Holmes. We waited for Woodley to collect himself.

'My mother was a Miss Gillies, born and brought up on St Kilda,' Woodley began. 'Few people ever visited that remote place, usually just fishermen from the other isles of the Hebrides, but there was one gentleman, a Dr Erasmus Woodley, from mainland Scotland, who was preparing a survey of the island. When he left, Miss Gillies went with him, and they were married. They settled in Yorkshire, where I was born. Later, I attended the University of London.

'In 1855 I undertook a tour of Scotland to observe bird life, and I thought to visit St Kilda, where my origins lay. There I met my grandmother, and also found I had an aunt and cousins there. On finding that I was interested in bird life, my grandmother told me a tale of a curious deformed bird she had seen very recently. When she described it, I knew at once that it had to be a great auk. I asked her to show me where she had seen it, and she told me she had killed it by striking it with an iron pan and thrown it on the fire. Imagine my distress, my disappointment at this loss. But as we know, great auks come ashore in pairs to lay their eggs and raise their young. Somewhere, I suspected, there had to be another, still searching for its mate. I told no-one of my intentions, but began to walk the island, looking for this bird. There was no hope of breeding from it, even had I been able to find another, as they mate for life. And at last, I did find it, a most unhappy wanderer amongst the rocks. There was no nest that I could see. So — what was I to do? I will not describe my actions, which pain me to this day. I was young — perhaps nowadays I might have acted differently. I don't know. I put the poor creature out of its misery. I warned my grandmother not to burn it, saying it was an important specimen, and I preserved it as well as I could using salt, which was all I had to hand. Lack of experience in these matters meant that I made a poor job of it. But I had heard tell of a respected collector who lived near Edinburgh, and on my way home I paid him a visit and sold the bird to him.'

'And this was, as you say, in the year 1855, when the great auk was already believed to be extinct?'

'It was only suspected it might be. Until some twenty years ago, we didn't know the true extent of the habitat of the great auk. They were most commonly seen south of the Arctic Circle, but that did not mean that they did not thrive further north, in regions where man rarely or never ventured. Many ornithologists believed that it was in fact primarily a bird of the

Arctic. We imagined, and I suppose we hoped, that the colonies we saw represented the southernmost reaches of their natural habitat. When the number of sightings dwindled, we found it hard to explain. Some men seized upon the works of Mr Darwin. Here was a bird which was by some principle finding it hard to exist, at least in those parts visited by men.

'But there was no reason for it that we could see. And so, the legend persisted, that what we had observed was only a small part of the total population, that somewhere further north was its natural, preferred breeding ground, where it liked to swim and feed. And if we were ever to go there, we would find great colonies, thousands of great auks in places where men could not live. When the numbers declined, we did not perceive that there was any fault in capturing specimens for collectors. There were men who studied the distribution of the auk population, but the results of their work were not published until about twenty years ago, some two years after my visit to St Kilda.

'It was only then that we knew that the waters south of the Arctic were the great auk's preferred territory and the legend of the great northern colonies was a myth, and the real reason why we saw the great auk no more was that it was extinct. And until then, we didn't know the truth. We just didn't know.' At this point Woodley became somewhat emotional and his eyes filled with tears.

Holmes and I looked at him silently until he managed to recover his composure.

'If that is the whole truth, then you have, as you say, committed no crime, no fraud,' said Holmes.

'But you see why I cannot reveal what I did? Why I dare not tell Professor Beare? There have been no accredited sightings of the great auk after mine. No breeding pairs since 1844.'

We said nothing but waited for him to continue.

'I have told you of my work for the protection of seabirds, a mission to which I have dedicated the last twenty years of my life. Imagine how humiliating it would be if my name were to be known not for that, but reviled throughout history as the man who killed the last great auk.'

'Did Charles Witwer Smith know or suspect your secret?' asked Holmes.

'I received a note from him. Professor Beare has not seen it, and I destroyed it. Smith wrote that he had spoken to Sir Andrew many years ago, shortly before he departed for New Zealand, and learned about a damaged specimen from St Kilda, and the difficulty in mounting it. That is why he thought it might be a partial skin only. When he saw it on display, he was sure it was the one Sir Andrew had spoken of. He was determined to visit St Kilda and learn more about how and when it was collected. I think he was driven by his hatred of Professor Owen and wanted to discredit him. My aunt and cousins still live in St Kilda. Had Smith gone there, he would undoubtedly have learned of my visit.'

'He must already have guessed your involvement,' said Holmes.

'Yes. Perhaps Sir Andrew made some mention of my name or appearance, I don't know.' Woodley put a hand to his luxuriant chestnut beard as he considered this. 'It must not have been enough of an indication for Smith to be certain, or he would have challenged me directly.'

'You had a motive to prevent him from going to St Kilda,' said Holmes.

'I — what? Prevent? What do you mean?' Woodley gasped. 'You surely can't think I would kill a man for such a reason?'

'Men have killed others for a few shillings,' said Holmes. 'You had a reputation to protect. And Smith's manner of death does resemble the means of collecting a flightless bird. However, my enquiries do confirm that at the time of Smith's death, you were attending a meeting at which a dozen others were present. And we have a description of the probable murderer which is very different from yours. I do not think you killed Charles Witwer Smith.'

Woodley uttered a groan of relief. 'What shall I do?' he said.

'It should be sufficient for the directors of the museum if you report to them that there is a note in Sir Andrew's diary that he purchased a preserved specimen of the great auk in 1855,' said Holmes. 'The date of collection is not mentioned. There have been unconfirmed sightings of great auks after 1844, so this would not be unreasonable. And there, I think, the matter should be left to lie. Any further publicity would not be in the best interests of the museum.'

Woodley agreed. What he told Professor Beare about his part in the matter I was never to learn. The disputed specimen of the great auk of St Kilda was never put on display again and remained in the museum's stores.

The building of Professor Owen's cherished second home of the British Museum was finally completed in 1880, and the task commenced of moving the natural history collection to the new location in South Kensington, a lengthy project meticulously overseen by Dr Woodley. The St Kilda great auk should have formed part of the great exodus, but strangely enough when the collections were next catalogued, it was absent. What became of it? If Holmes ever solved that mystery, he kept the answer to himself.

CHAPTER TWENTY-EIGHT

'It is a fine day,' said Holmes to me when I next saw him. 'You might assist me on a little expedition which I hope will prove both pleasurable and informative.' He saw me look doubtful about this description, since in my experience Holmes's expeditions, while usually informative, were occasionally dangerous and far from pleasurable. He smiled. 'We are about to take a stroll in the sunshine with an elderly lady.'

Naturally I agreed. I wasn't sure to whom Holmes could be referring, and wondered if the lady might be a venerable relative of his. If so, I might learn something about Holmes's antecedents, a subject to which he rarely referred. It was also an opportunity for me to acquire experience of taking care of a lady of advanced years, which would be valuable when I had my own medical practice.

To my surprise, I found myself accompanying Holmes to the square where Mrs Smith resided. His destination, however, was the house next door, Walnut Villa. The maid who opened the door to his knock was clearly expecting us and showed us in, where we were received by Mrs Bailey.

'Oh, Mr Holmes, Mr Stamford,' she exclaimed. 'I am so glad you have called; how very thoughtful of you. Aunt Jane is having one of her days. She has been fretting so and will like to have company.'

'I thought she might enjoy a little walk in the sunshine,' said Holmes. 'It is pleasantly warm for the time of year.'

'She doesn't go very far nowadays, of course, but she does like to sit in the gardens when she can.'

'Then we will be delighted to accompany her there,' said Holmes.

Aunt Jane was not averse to this expedition, especially when she saw she would be leaning on the arms of two young gentlemen. Some time was required to prepare her, and ensure she had the right shawls and wraps and boots and mittens for the outdoors, but at last we were able to support her as far as the door and assist her down the steps. The roadway was free of all traffic, and we crossed over at a suitable pace to the gate of the gardens.

'Do you have a favourite bench where you like to sit?' asked Holmes, kindly.

'It is that one,' she said, pointing at a bench to our left as we passed through the entrance.

'Ah, that is a very convenient place,' said Holmes. 'From there you may gaze upon the flower beds, benefit from the shade of a tree, and enjoy an excellent view of the villas and any visitors.'

'I like to see who comes and goes,' said Aunt Jane, with a throaty chuckle. 'There's been too much of it round here just lately.'

We sat down on the bench indicated.

'Did you happen to see anything on the day Professor Smith met with his unfortunate end?' asked Holmes. 'It was January, so I expect you were not sitting here but staying warm indoors. Although you might be able to see a great deal from the front window, too.'

'I heard all the commotion,' she said. 'I'm not so deaf as people suppose. I heard Mrs Smith cry out, all of a sudden, "Oh no!" or something like that, and I did look out, but there was nothing to be seen, and then about a minute after, she started up good and proper, "Help! Murder!"'

'Were you able to see people coming and going after that?' asked Holmes.

'People ran out from their houses into the street when the screaming started, but there were no menfolk about, so no-one went in to help Mrs Smith until the coal man arrived and broke in.'

'Mr Bailey had already left for his office?'

'Oh yes, prompt on the hour. All weathers. Very proud of that, he is.'

'Did you see anyone leave?'

'No, not by the front door, at any rate. I thought at first there must be robbers in the house, so they might have run out the back. Then the doctor came, and all the police. And the coal man climbed out and the police congratulated him.' She leaned towards Holmes with a confiding look. 'You know that young man calls there, don't you?'

'So I have heard.'

'People think I don't see anything, but when he passes by on his coal cart the maid looks out of the window, and they wave to each other and blow kisses. He wouldn't be allowed in the house in his working clothes. But I have seen them walking out together when he is respectably dressed, and they seem very affectionate. And he calls round for tea on Sunday afternoons, all in his church clothes and carrying a posy of flowers. He doesn't come to the front door, of course, but I see him in the street, and he takes the path round to the kitchen door. And I shouldn't say it, but he stays in the house a lot longer than he ought to. There. That is all I have to say about that.'

This seemed a little indelicate, and Holmes declined to pursue the subject in more detail.

'Are there many callers to Park Villa?' he asked. 'I mean, in general, not just on the day Professor Smith died.'

'Not many. Deliveries go to the kitchen door. Professor Smith never had anyone call, apart from Dr Scales from time to time. Mrs Roper, that's Mrs Smith's sister, she comes. And a young friend of Mr Charles Smith, he used to call after Mr Charles came home.'

'That would be Mr Selby,' I said.

'I never knew his name.'

'Did you ever speak to Mr Smith or see him in the company of another person?' I asked.

'No, the poor young man, I never did. He was always busy with his work.'

'And Professor Smith?'

'I saw him in the street sometimes, and at church, of course, but he was never inclined to talk much. He used to hold his head and shake it.' She tapped the side of her head. 'There was something wrong up there.'

'You must have spoken to Mrs Smith on occasion,' said Holmes.

'Oh yes, she always greeted me very friendly after church, and we had a little talk, just to pass the time.'

'Did she ever complain about the behaviour of the maid?'

'Complain? No. She never said anything about her.'

'She was remarkably tolerant of the coal man's visits to Miss Jenny. Another employer would have dismissed her for such behaviour.'

To our surprise, Aunt Jane uttered a hoarse laugh. 'That woman is an old fool,' she said. 'She ought to have known better.'

'What do you mean?'

'I mean she never said so, but I can always tell these things. I saw her, Mrs Smith, looking out of the window as he went past in his cart, turning her head to follow him. She had a soft spot herself for the young man, didn't she? That's why she allowed him to call. He came to see the maid, but she might have thought or hoped he had another object.'

'A puzzle may have many pieces,' said Holmes, once we had safely delivered Aunt Jane to her home and proceeded on our way. 'To solve it, one must locate and identify every small fragment, however unimportant they might appear, and finally assemble them correctly, in order to form a picture.'

'Do you have the picture now?' I asked.

'Not quite, but it is merely a matter of time.' He paused, suddenly. 'Yes, of course, time; not only the events, but also the order in which they occurred.'

'I would be interested to know your conclusions,' I said.

'I promise you shall hear them,' said Holmes. 'In the meantime, I invite you to imagine what the immediate consequences would have been if Alastair Caldie had succeeded in murdering his sister with the adulterated medicine.'

I was always concerned when Holmes asked me questions of this sort, as I knew my answers would never satisfy him. I thought about what actions Miss Caldie's doctor would have taken, and what his suspicions might have been. 'I suppose the medicine bottle would have been examined soon afterwards and the arsenic found. The police would have known it was a case of murder.'

'And who would they have suspected?'

'Whoever had the opportunity to add the arsenic and would have benefitted from the crime.'

'Precisely,' said Holmes. 'Miss Mercer stood to benefit very substantially from Miss Caldie's will, and she knew of it since she was the executor. Not only would she have enjoyed a lifetime of financial security and independence, but her position would have allowed her control over the Caldie Society and the bulk of Miss Caldie's fortune. Miss Mercer collected the bottle from the chemist and gave Miss Caldie the first dose. There is no record of her having purchased arsenic, but people have been known to do so under a false name. Mr Caldie, since he did not benefit from his sister's death, would not have been a suspect.'

'But he thought he would benefit,' I said.

'That,' said Holmes, 'is my very point.' He said no more and was not seen at Barts again that day or anywhere else for that matter. I rather think he went back to his rooms in Montague Street to smoke his pipe.

CHAPTER TWENTY-NINE

'Have you deduced who murdered Charles Smith?' was my first question to Holmes when we next sat down to a simple supper of meat pie and boiled potatoes in my rooms.

He smiled. 'One thing at a time,' he said. 'To consider the position in the Smith household, we must go back further, to a time when Smith was still in New Zealand.'

I saw that Holmes wanted to address the mystery in his own way at his own pace. It was not exactly that he enjoyed the sound of his own voice, although I sometimes suspected that he did, but the very act of expounding his insights to another assisted his deliberations. I know I did give Holmes some assistance in his enquiries, but my main function was to listen, and reflect his thoughts back to him. I attended to my supper and opened a bottle of beer.

'When I read of the death of Professor Smith and then saw the house, I was struck by a number of considerations,' Holmes began. 'First of all, the location. Who would have heard Mrs Smith screaming murder? Who was able to go to her assistance if they heard her cries? Park Villa was the last in the row. In Walnut Villa, the adjacent house, Mr Bailey, the only man who might have been called upon to intervene, was a man of regular habits. He had already breakfasted and departed for his office in the city. The other inhabitants, Mrs Bailey, her aunt, the cook, and the maid, would not have entered a house where murder was being done. On the opposite side of the road, there were no houses facing, only gardens.

'Then there was the time when the event occurred, which was attended by a number of apparent coincidences. Not only the predictable absence of Mr Bailey, but the maid, Jenny, the only person who lived with Professor and Mrs Smith, had just been sent on an errand to fetch milk. And the incident occurred at the very moment that the coal delivery man, Mr Hepden, was passing, and was able to intervene to save Mrs Smith.

'No-one could have known that the coal man would be there at that exact moment,' I said.

'On the contrary, Mrs Smith would have clearly heard the sound of the coal going into the cellar, which told her he was in the vicinity. If she knew his usual route, which I am sure she did, she would have been aware that he would be passing the house very shortly afterwards.'

'That is true,' I said. I was far from understanding where Holmes's deliberations were going. It is not usually advisable to interrupt him, although saying something foolish often provokes a response.

'When I first spoke to Mrs Bailey,' Holmes continued, 'my concerns were intensified. None of these circumstances were proof of any crime, but taken together they were extremely suggestive. I felt increasingly certain that Professor Smith had not killed himself but had in fact been murdered. The only questions to determine, therefore, are how, why and by whom. I have made further enquiries and Sergeant Lestrade was able to confirm that the bloodstained razor found at the scene was Professor Smith's own razor, and it was normally kept by the washstand in the upstairs bedroom where he shaved each morning. He also confirmed that the police made thorough searches of the house and found no signs of an intruder.'

Holmes was rarely wrong, and I feared that this was not one of those occasions. 'The only other person in the room was Mrs Smith,' I protested. 'Are you saying that she killed her husband? If so, it must have been when defending herself from his attack. Perhaps she somehow wrested the razor from him and didn't want to admit it. Many of the scars on her hands are very deep, and I doubt that she would have inflicted them upon herself.'

'Mrs Smith did not kill her husband, neither did she make those deep cuts. But she knows who did.'

'You mean — she is shielding the killer?'

'She is.'

'I don't understand. Why would she do such a thing?'

Holmes looked at me with a raised eyebrow, as if to remonstrate with me for being so obtuse. 'You already have all the facts, Stamford,' he said.

'The location — the timing —' I said. 'Are you saying it was all a plan? A murder made to look like a suicide? By someone who entered and left without leaving a trace? By the kitchen door, I suppose. And given Professor Smith's erratic behaviour and melancholy, as described by Dr Scales, no-one would question the official verdict. Is Mrs Smith shielding the killer because he or possibly even she was her co-conspirator?'

'That is what I believe. Which led me to consider that the scene in the breakfast room was not as it seemed. Mrs Smith had undoubtedly suffered some very unpleasant injuries. A few of the cuts were not very deep, but others were. She bled considerably. There were spots of blood spattered up the wall in streams where they had been thrown off the blade of the razor. A savage attack by another individual. But there was no sign of her having run away to avoid her attacker. The blood that fell to the carpet made round drops, which suggested that after being cut she did not move.'

I thought again. 'The coal man, Mr Hepden, supported Mrs Smith's story, so he must have been involved. He heard her screaming and broke in and — did he commit the murder?' I stopped. 'But when he broke in, Mrs Smith had already been screaming murder for some little while. And we know that Professor Smith was not under the influence of alcohol or any soporific. He was fully conscious. Surely, he would not have sat there quietly at the breakfast table while his wife screamed murder?'

'He did not,' said Holmes. 'When Mr Hepden broke into the house, Professor Smith was already dead.'

I was inevitably rather confused by this, and Holmes allowed me some moments to consider the implications. 'Hepden said that Professor Smith was attacking his wife when he burst in, and only killed himself when he rescued Mrs Smith,' I said. 'If what you say is true, then both Hepden and Mrs Smith must have lied at the inquest. Did Mrs Smith offer to pay Hepden, if not to actually commit the murder then to be a witness? He might have needed money if he was courting the maid, and I imagine that a coal carrier does not receive a great wage.' I tried my hardest to find some thread of truth. 'Someone must have connived with Mrs Smith to murder Professor Smith. Perhaps someone who was already visiting. And whoever that person was must have run away through the back door without leaving any sign that they were there. And the maid being out on an errand, having been sent out by Mrs Smith, I suppose, would not have seen anyone. Then Mr Hepden breaks in and Mrs Smith is able to bribe him to support her story. Is that what happened?'

Holmes smiled. 'Let us look at it another way. The question one must ask is, who gains? Or — and this was the point I made before, when discussing Mr Caldie — who thought they would gain, even if they were mistaken? People do not always act upon what the true situation is, but what they believe to be true.'

I agreed but was unable to offer any comment. Our supper continued in contemplative silence.

'Consider this,' said Holmes. 'When a wife kills her husband, she has three possible motives. One is that he is a brute and she wishes to be rid of him. There is no evidence of that, although much can be hidden behind closed doors. The only thing we can say is that Professor Smith's behaviour had given cause for disquiet in recent months. Mrs Smith and their son attributed this to his despondency over his professional standing, which they blamed on Professor Owen. My conversation with Dr Scales suggested that there might have been another cause. In time, this might have advanced to the point where he was required to be confined for his own protection, but it is not a motive for murder. The second motive is that the wife has a beau whom she prefers to her husband and whom she wishes to take his place. Murder can often be regarded as a more convenient alternative to legal processes. It is quicker, and less expensive. Did Mrs Smith have an admirer she wished to marry? The only male callers at the house were Mr Hepden, who is less than half her age and is courting the maid, and Dr Scales and Mr Selby, both of whom are married. The third motive is money. Usually, we find in such cases that the deceased has been insured, or that he has left his murderer a substantial inheritance. Neither of these considerations existed here. Mrs Smith did not inherit the bulk of her husband's property and was not left in a financially better position on his death. Rather the opposite, in fact. But as we have recently learned, until her husband's will was proved, she was under the impression that he had, as she requested, bequeathed her the house. And she had no idea that he had gone into debt to finance his fossil collection.'

'Then the motive was money?'

'It was. And the murder had to be carried out before Charles Smith arrived in England to take charge of his father, or Dr Scales ordered the professor to be confined to an asylum. Either of these situations would have placed the professor out of reach of his murderers. Mrs Smith had written to her son advising him of her husband's indisposition, possibly to prepare him for the worst, but she might not have expected him to sail home. If Professor Smith was to die, it had to be done without too much delay.'

'But Mrs Smith had been promised by her husband that she would always have a roof over her head,' I pointed out. 'Even if the son owned the property, she still had the right to live there. Her life would have gone on as before. She didn't need to arrange her husband's death.'

'Only if she remained single. Whatever rights she might have had would have expired on any remarriage. It was essential to Professor Smith, whatever his wife's protestations, that the property should pass directly to his son on his death. He lied about the will in order to placate her.'

'I am not sure I follow you,' I said.

'You recall what Mrs Bailey's Aunt Jane said? She is often dismissed as a gossip, but I sense an astute understanding of human nature, and an experienced observer. She said that Mrs Smith might have entertained the foolish hope that Mr Hepden actually called to see her, even though he appeared to come to see the maid. And Dr Scales said that one of Professor Smith's delusions concerned the behaviour of his wife. Usually a delusion is just that, but sometimes there is an underlying truth.'

'Mr Hepden?'

'I can't prove it, but I think he might have played upon Mrs Smith's affections, and convinced her that his supposed association with the maid was just a ruse to protect her reputation and conceal his real interests. What he was actually seeking was a widow with a value to which he in his humble occupation could never aspire. But when the will was proved, it became apparent that the scheme had failed.'

'But you are sure that Mrs Smith did not murder her husband?'

'Yes, the hand that cut the professor's throat and her arms so deeply was not the same one that made the shallow cuts.'

'Then whose?'

'The one person we cannot safely ignore is the maid, Jenny. Yes, she was sent on an errand supposedly to enable the crime to be committed without a witness, and the police have established without any doubt that she was not in the house when the murder occurred. You have suggested that this was a part of the plan, but let us go further — what if she was complicit? Once we assume young Jenny's involvement, the picture becomes much clearer. Her association with Hepden was genuine, her desire for money the same as his. They planned it together, and Mrs Smith was their victim, valued only for her financial worth, and cruelly wooed into being a part of it. Had the scheme worked, and had Mrs Smith married Hepden, her property would have fallen under his control, and sooner or later he would have found a way to become owner of it all.'

'He would have murdered her?'

'I believe so. And then he and the maid would have married, and much joy the two cold-blooded murderers would have had of each other's company.'

'Holmes — who killed Professor Smith? You said it was not Mrs Smith or Mr Hepden. And the maid was not there.'

'Ah,' said Holmes, wistfully. 'You hear but you do not understand. I said that Professor Smith was already dead when Hepden broke in. I did not say that Hepden did not kill him.'

CHAPTER THIRTY

I was as mystified as ever and could only wait, while we completed our supper, to hear Holmes's deductions.

'I feel sure that Hepden and Jenny were in collusion,' said Holmes, as he laid down his knife and fork. 'In fact, I would not be surprised to find that hers was the mind behind the plan. She was in a position to overhear the conversations between Mrs Smith and her sister. She learned that Mrs Smith was not happy with her husband, whose erratic behaviour was giving cause for concern. She might even have heard Mrs Smith say that she feared that he would lay violent hands on himself. And, most importantly, Mrs Smith must have told her sister that she would inherit the house and a valuable fossil collection on her husband's death.

'On the morning of the murder, Hepden called at the back door and Jenny let him in. He was in his working clothes, so it was essential that he left no trace of coal dust in those parts of the house where he ought not to be. A maidservant is very well placed to know about dirt and dust. She had laid newspapers, the ones she normally kept for lighting the fires, along the length of the carpet so he would not leave marks on the floor. I expect she warned him not to touch anything outside the breakfast room. She showed him to the door of that room, turned the handle and pushed it open without being seen or heard. The door hinges, which I examined, had been liberally oiled in the last few months. He walked in, approached the professor from behind and cut his throat. Even though Mrs Smith was expecting it, it shocked her, and she exclaimed loudly enough for Aunt Jane to hear. That was the first cry of

"Oh no!" Once the deed was done, Hepden left the house, still without leaving a mark, and Jenny closed the door, gathered up the dirty papers and burnt them in the kitchen range. I am sure Mrs Smith was far too distracted to notice that the maid was still in the house. Jenny left very soon afterwards to establish her alibi. Hepden then proceeded in his coal wagon. But he did make two mistakes.'

This was the point where Holmes liked to make a significant pause during which he lit his pipe, but knowing I cannot abide tobacco smoke he had to be content with addressing the few remaining crumbs of pastry on his supper plate.

'Matters became clear to me when I was able to examine the breakfast room,' Holmes went on. 'The position of the blood spots by the fireplace, which I have already mentioned, and also spots behind the chair where the professor had been seated at the breakfast table. His killer came up behind him, seized him around the shoulders, tilted him back and in one movement, cut his throat. Such boldness. Such cruelty. I would not be surprised to find that the murderer had once worked in a slaughterhouse. That is the reason for the absence of the classic hesitation cuts of the suicide, which Dr Scales noted. The body then fell to the floor where it was found. There was no outburst over a journal. I noted the name and edition of the torn matter on the table and when I was able to examine a copy, I found the contents quite innocuous. I expect it was placed there by Mrs Smith from her husband's collection.'

'How did Hepden get hold of the professor's razor?' I asked. 'He can't have gone upstairs.'

'He didn't. My theory is that he used his own, which he brought to the scene in his pocket. He may have stood there for a few seconds after the deadly cut, during which blood dripped to the floor. But he needed to take the weapon away with him, so, without thinking, he picked up a napkin from the table, wiped the blade, wrapped the razor in the material and put it in his pocket. You recall that there was only one napkin on the table. That was why I asked Mrs Roper to count them. One of the set of six was missing.'

'But the professor's razor was found in the room, with blood on it.'

'Yes. I think Mrs Smith had been told to conceal it somewhere in the breakfast room. It might even have been in her pocket. When the time came, she was to cut herself to make it look as if she had been attacked. That was the origin of the small cuts and the slight spots on the carpet. Mrs Smith then screamed out "Help! Murder!" to attract attention. After Hepden broke in he saw that she had been faint-hearted about the cuts, which is understandable, and he took the razor from her to make some more convincing ones. And that was when she screamed in good earnest.'

'How horrible! And you think he planned to marry her, then murder her and marry the maid?'

'I believe so.'

'But then he found that it had all been in vain.'

'He did.'

'Can any of this be proved?'

'I doubt it. I expect Hepden, when he arrived home, cleaned the razor and burnt the napkin. Any residue of blood he might have missed is easily accounted for. Blood splashes on his clothes may also be explained by his intrusion on the scene, as would coal dust in the breakfast room and on the professor's clothing. The blood drops, the missing napkin — I doubt that is sufficient for a prosecution. What is needed is a full confession from Mrs Smith.'

'Unlikely,' I said.

'I think,' said Holmes, 'I know how that might be procured.'

At this point Holmes stood and started pacing the room impatiently, looking at his watch. 'I know who killed Charles Smith and why,' he said. 'I am right, I am sure of it, but a court of law will require evidence. I have told Lestrade my reasoning and where that evidence is to be found. He must act quickly, before the culprit suspects discovery and absconds. I am hoping that his recent successes after taking my advice will encourage him to follow up my suggestion. I am waiting for him to call.'

'What evidence is this?' I asked.

'The one thing that links the murderer with the crime. The trinket box stolen from the body. I have told Lestrade where to find it, and I hope that he is carrying out my wishes.'

I sensed Holmes's frustration. How he must have wanted to dash to wherever he knew the evidence would be and uncover it with a flourish to the astonished eyes of the police, to be greeted with a round of applause. When he became a celebrated and world-famous detective, he blithely ignored established procedures with impunity, but had he done so as a twenty-three-year-old student, he would probably have been arrested.

'Once Hepden saw that there was no real advantage to marrying Mrs Smith, he might have decided to give up on the plan, but he and his *inamorata* must have been frustrated to see the prize slip away from them. Charles Smith was young and in good health. Not only that, but he was planning to return to New Zealand and marry. That, I am afraid, was why they determined to murder him. If he died unmarried, the family property would pass to his next of kin, his mother. Their one chance was escaping, and they had to act quickly.'

'Mrs Smith can't have been involved in that?'

'I am sure she knew nothing of it. And how she might feel if she ever suspected that she had brought this fate on her son, one can hardly imagine.'

It was a long wait, but eventually we received a visit from Lestrade, who announced that the trinket box had been discovered hidden in the belongings of the Smiths' family maid, Jenny Jay. The police had arrested both the maid and Samuel Hepden and had charged them with the murder of Charles Smith.

Jenny Jay was later identified by a pawnbroker as the young woman who had pawned a watch, which was shown by its markings to be that belonging to Charles Smith. The role of Hepden and Jenny in the death of Professor Smith was never established. It would hardly have benefitted either of them to claim in their defence that they had been hired by Mrs Smith to murder her husband. Since Mrs Smith had gained nothing by her husband's death, a court would have thrown out that claim. The professor's violent death was consequently assumed to be what it had appeared to be, a suicide. Dr Scales, out of consideration for the professor's memory, wrote a letter to the *Times* explaining his theory that his patient had not been insane but had suffered from a tumour of the brain.

It was Samuel Hepden alone who eventually stood trial for the murder of Charles Smith. There was no evidence to convince a jury that Jenny Jay was involved in the planning or commission of the crime. Holmes believed that the maid's knowledge of Charles Smith's movements had assisted Hepden in his plan to follow him, but that could not be proven. The maid had no compunction about sacrificing her lover to save herself by turning Queen's evidence. She told the court that the pawning of the watch had been done at the request of Hepden, to whom she was betrothed. She also claimed that the trinket box had been a gift, and she was shocked when she learned of its origins.

Samuel Hepden was found guilty of the murder of Charles Smith and sentenced to death. Jenny Jay witnessed his condemnation unmoved.

Holmes was extremely unhappy that he had not been able to find a means to convict the very person whom he was convinced had initiated the entire murderous scheme. 'The law assumes that in the absence of evidence to the contrary, the woman must be subordinate to the man, and acting under his direction, even duress,' he said. 'This is not always the case, and I believe that a dangerous woman has been set free. Once a criminal has found how easy it is to evade the law, he or she will see it as an open door, *carte blanche* to continue in the same manner.'

Despite this disappointment, Holmes did not list the case amongst those he later described to Watson as his 'failures'. Failure to Holmes meant he had been unable to discover the truth. The process of the law was beyond his remit.

Holmes remained certain that one day Miss Jenny Jay would expose her true nature through overconfidence and finally be punished as she deserved. He knew her methods and would look out for them in future. But I will leave that story for another time.

Mrs Smith was never tried for any crime but existed in a prison of her own making. Unable to face the world, she lived out the remainder of her days with her sister, under the care of a nurse.

CHAPTER THIRTY-ONE

I had anticipated that Miss Caldie would publish a pamphlet announcing to the world that the accusations made by Charles Smith regarding her grandfather's great auk had been proven to be misguided, and it was now accepted by authorities in the field to be a genuine specimen. This pamphlet never appeared. I guessed that on reflection, and taking note of comments made by Holmes, she had decided to let the whole affair fade into obscurity where it might rest forgotten. Should anyone ever refer to the accusation, she knew that she could simply direct them to the superintendent of natural history at the British Museum, but it appears that she never needed to do so.

I thought we were to hear no more from Miss Caldie, but I unexpectedly received a note from her asking me to call in order to discuss an important business matter. The Caldie Society had been launched, and funds from interested parties were flowing in. I assumed that our meeting must be in connection with that enterprise.

Miss Caldie received me in her drawing room, where she was looking even more serious than usual. I had thought that Holmes, too, would be in attendance, but he was not. I was even more surprised to see that Miss Mercer was not present.

'You know, of course, that I have vowed to devote to my life to education,' she said.

'A most worthy object,' I said. 'I expect you will be founding schools and perhaps even one day a university.'

'That is the purpose of the Caldie Society. For myself, personally, I wish to focus my influence on a small group of young persons over whom I have complete control. It is therefore my intention to have charge of a family, the better to guide and develop the children from the moment of birth. The girls will receive a thorough education, as good as any that currently exists. The boys also, and they will be taught to respect women and acknowledge them as equals.'

'Then you intend to adopt some orphans?' I said. It was not an unusual object for a single lady of fortune, although I was not sure how I was to assist. Perhaps, I thought, she wished me to be a sponsor of the scheme. 'That is very charitable, very commendable.'

'I do not,' she said tersely. 'One can never be sure of their forebears. There may be bad blood in the families that will only become apparent later in life.'

I was not at all sure where this conversation was tending and thought it safer to say nothing.

'This ambition can only be realised if I marry,' she said.

I nodded as if to imply understanding, but truly I still could not see how I might be involved. Was she asking me for recommendations?

'Your friend, Mr Holmes,' she continued.

'Oh dear!' I exclaimed under my breath, as her intentions had now become clear, but I had spoken rather louder than I imagined.

She heard my words and paused, with a hard stare. 'Your friend, Mr Holmes,' she repeated, in a sharper tone, 'is a highly intelligent man of good family, and yes, I did consider him for the role of husband. However, on reflection, I felt that he would be difficult to mould to my wishes.'

'Ah,' I said, with an exhalation of relief.

'You, on the other hand, Mr Stamford, are both intelligent and malleable. I have made enquiries and have established that you are single, without attachments, and there are no flaws to be found in your family.'

It took a few moments for the import of this statement to become apparent to me. It took a little longer for me to find my voice, which, when it emerged, did not sound like mine at all, but like that of a frightened mouse with its tail caught in a trap.

'Do you think that a good idea?'

'I do, or I would not have mentioned it.'

'I — er — I am very poor, you know.'

She shrugged off my objection. 'That is no matter, as I have an ample fortune. It will be necessary, of course, to place a significant portion in trust before we marry, to reserve it for my personal use.'

'My father is a cabinet maker!'

Miss Caldie smiled. 'Having a carpenter as one's father is no bar to greatness.'

'I have taken a vow never to marry!' I exclaimed. I hadn't, but it did seem like a good time to do so.

She waved away that obstacle. 'As I did once, before I saw the necessity.'

'And even if I wanted to, I could not marry for very many years. I have my studies to complete.'

'And you shall complete them. Mr Stamford, or may I call you Arthur? I will place no hindrance in the way of your education as long as you are an attentive husband. So, I believe that is settled. Might I suggest a formal announcement soon and a wedding to take place in the autumn? Let us seal our agreement with a handshake. I do not require anything further at this point in time.'

I was gripped by terror. The prospect of 'anything further' was like a sickly weight in my stomach. She rose from her chair and approached me, offering her hand, and I was seized with a strong desire to run away. I tried desperately to think of some hardened criminal in my family who would place me beyond the pale, but both sides from which I was descended were determinedly honest. And then I perceived my route of escape.

'Your brother!' I gasped.

Her face hardened. 'I have no brother.'

'And yet you are related by blood to a would-be murderer of his own sister. A gambler, a drunkard, a libertine, and who knows what else. Miss Caldie, I am truly honoured and flattered that you have selected me as a suitable match. Had things been different, then I would see no impediment to our union. But I cannot accept an offer which would place me as a relation to Mr Caldie.'

She gazed back at me silently and I could see that my words had touched her deeply. 'Yes,' she said at last. 'I fear you may be right. I am sorry to have inconvenienced and embarrassed you, Mr Stamford. I wish you good day.'

I bade her farewell as courteously as I could, with all my good wishes for her future. It was a future we knew we would never share. Then I left.

CHAPTER THIRTY-TWO

I was congratulating Holmes on his recent successes when he interrupted me. 'Has it occurred to you, Stamford, that there is a larger mystery to be solved here, and a far more important one than might be supposed?'

I decided not to try and guess what that might be, and merely asked to be enlightened.

'Why did the great auk become extinct?' he said. 'Let us consider the various possibilities. If the bird had lived in just one part of the world, and that part was obliterated by some natural phenomenon, that would be an explanation, but its home was the sea and it ranged widely in the northern waters. Did its food supply fail? It did not. Its food was the vast richness of the ocean. It swam swiftly and caught its prey with ease. It was eminently suited to feed in that way. Did it have natural enemies? No more than any other creature. Has the climate of the earth become unfriendly to it? There is no evidence of that. What of man the predator? The auk came to remote islands once a year, staying briefly to lay eggs and rear its young, places that are either wholly unpopulated by man or support very small communities who do not have the leisure to kill simply for sport. The taking of birds or their eggs for food for a short period of time by so few people would not have destroyed colonies of thousands. The very remoteness of the great auk's breeding grounds protected them from hunters who found targets for their guns much closer to home. And yet, when men of science went to those islands where great auks were known to congregate in vast numbers, with the object of studying their habits, they were shocked to find only the remains of what had once been a thriving species. Ornithologists themselves, eager to obtain specimens of a rare bird for their collections, have been blamed for the disappearance, but that was only the final insult to a population which was already greatly declined. Professor Darwin himself would be at a loss to apply his famous principle to the extinction of such a bird. What are we to make of it?'

'Professors Beare and Newton might be correct,' I said. 'There might still be great auks in more northerly regions.'

'If there are, they have not yet been seen, and since we now know it is not their preferred habitat, even if they were to be found, we still have the question of what drove them there. But you understand my thinking?' Holmes hardly paused for a reply. 'Professor Newton wrote in his journal, the *Ibis*, that science should study recent extinctions in order to better understand ancient ones, but I would take it further than that. If a successful species such as the great auk can disappear in a short time for no reason that we can as yet discover, then what other species may join them in oblivion in the future? Birds, reptiles, mammals, even man himself. The extinction of a flightless bird might seem to be a trivial question, but if we can answer it, what might we discover that we could use to ensure our own continued existence?'

At this, Holmes fell silent, and I saw him gazing into the far distance to that unknown future, the promise of which only he could see.

HISTORICAL NOTES

By 1877 most scholars had accepted that the great auk was extinct, but the reasons for this were not fully understood. The most detailed account of the extinction of the great auk is *Who Killed the Great Auk?* by Jeremy Gaskell (Oxford University Press, 2000) to which I am greatly indebted.

I am also indebted to Alison Leech of the Natural History Museum for additional information.

I have consulted nineteenth-century works, my intention being to provide the spirit and viewpoints of the time, rather than imposing a modern perspective. We now know that the decline of the great auk was due to organised commercial hunting when, over many years, for several weeks during the breeding season, the birds were killed in large numbers for meat, oil and the soft down of their breast feathers.

I have consulted contemporary works on bird collection and preservation, notably *Bird-preserving, bird-mounting, and the preservation of birds' eggs* by Richard Avis (1870, London, Groombridge and Sons) and *The naturalist's guide in collecting and preserving objects of natural history: with a complete catalogue of the birds of the eastern Massachusetts* by C. J. Maynard, (S. E. Cassino, Salem, Massachusetts, 1877).

A warning — I have studied nineteenth-century medical and surgical textbooks which made pleasanter reading.

Professor Sir Richard Owen (1804–1892) was one of the leading naturalists of his day, famous for coining the word *Dinosauria*. He often attracted controversy as a critic of Darwin's theory of natural selection and was accused of taking credit for the work of others. One of his greatest achievements was a successful campaign for a dedicated museum to be provided for the zoological and botanical specimens originally housed in the British Museum.

The British Museum (Natural History) began construction in 1873 and was opened to the public in 1881. The removal of the natural history collection to its new home was not completed until 1883. It became formally known as the Natural History Museum in 1992.

For more information on Owen's life and career see *The Dinosaur Hunters* by Deborah Cadbury (Fourth Estate, 2001).

Alfred Newton (1829–1907) was Professor of Zoology and Comparative Anatomy at Cambridge University. He suffered an injury as a child which left one leg shorter than the other. He was a leading founder of the British Ornithologists Union in 1858 and its journal, the *Ibis*, in the following year. His interest in extinct species led him to campaign for the conservation of birds. He visited Iceland in 1858 hoping to find evidence of living great auks, but did not, although he continued to hope that they might be found. His observations on the great auk may be found in the October 1861 edition of the *Ibis*, pp. 374–399:
https://archive.org/details/ibis03brit/page/374/mode/2up

The character of Miss Caldie is inspired by Lydia Ernestine Becker (1827–1890) who campaigned energetically for women's suffrage and advocated non-gendered education. At the annual meeting of the British Association in August 1868, Professor Newton blamed ladies for the destruction of gulls for their feathers, telling every lady present that they wore upon their foreheads the 'brand of a murderer' (*Gloucester*

Journal, 29 August 1868, p. 3). Miss Becker responded that ladies should not be held responsible, but should be instructed on this and other subjects, and placed the blame on men for keeping women in ignorance, a speech for which she was applauded. Professor Newton did not return to the fray. (*Huntley Express*, 29 August 1868, p. 2).
https://en.wikipedia.org/wiki/Lydia_Becker

The *Natural History Review* is fictional.

The moa, a flightless bird of New Zealand, became extinct around 1445. Prior to human settlement its only predator was Haast's eagle. Human settlers drove the moa to extinction by hunting and forest clearance in less than a hundred years. As a result, Haast's eagle, which relied on the moa for food, also became extinct.

The Seabirds Preservation Act became law in 1869.

The Papa Westray great auk is in the research collection of the Natural History Museum, Tring.
 A specimen of the great auk is one of the treasures in the Cadogan Gallery at the Natural History Museum, London. Believed to have been collected in Iceland in 1837, it was acquired by the museum in 1937 as part of the Baron Rothschild bequest.
https://www.nhm.ac.uk/visit/galleries-and-museum-map/treasures-in-the-cadogan-gallery.html

The last accepted sighting of a great auk was in 1852. Sir Andrew Caldie's great auk is, of course, fictitious.

The 'squalid incident' at Harvard Medical College alluded to by Holmes is the Parkman–Webster case of 1849.

Camomile Street still exists but the nineteenth-century buildings are long gone. The Mailcoach Inn and the Saracen's Head appear on the 1881 census, as does a coffee house. The office of the New Zealand shipping company was at 84 Bishopsgate Street.

In *The Adventure of the Greek Interpreter* Holmes reveals his ancestry to Watson. The country squires are not named. There were three painters named Vernet, three generations of the same line, but given their dates the most probable one to be Holmes's great uncle was Emile Jean Horace (1789–1863).

The Royal Society for the Protection of Birds originates from movements formed in 1889 by two groups of women who campaigned against the wanton destruction of birds for their feathers, and the use of feathers in fashion. Professor Alfred Newton became a supporter.

William Cameron (1829–1902) was a Scottish-born tobacco manufacturer with factories in the Unites States and from the 1870s, Australia.

Holmes is described as '…a strange, lank bird, with dull grey plumage and a black top-knot' (*The Adventure of the Dancing Men*). Presumably the clothes were grey and the hair black — a rare reference by Watson to the colour of Holmes's hair.

Holmes in his comments on Canterbury Cathedral is undoubtedly referring to the assassination of 'turbulent priest'

Thomas à Becket.

The passenger pigeon (*Ectopistes migratorius*) was cited in the nineteenth century as an example of the resilience of a bird population to hunting. Its numbers had declined considerably by 1890 and it was extinct in the wild by the early twentieth century. The last example died in a zoo in 1914.

Bewick's *History of British Birds* may be consulted online: https://archive.org/details/historyofbritish00bewi/page/150/mode/2up

A NOTE TO THE READER

The timeline of the events in the life of Sherlock Holmes in the canonical fifty-six stories and four novels has occupied, fascinated and sometimes frustrated Holmesian scholars for many years. The most commonly accepted year of Holmes's birth is 1854. He did not meet Dr Watson and occupy 221b Baker Street before 1881.

Almost nothing is known about his early life and very little about his education. I think it is possible that, like Conan Doyle, he spent a year at school on the continent, where he acquired his knowledge of modern languages. He is known to have spent two years at a collegiate university, which means either Oxford or Cambridge, although which one, and what courses he took have never been revealed, but he did not take a degree. The year in which he settled permanently in London is unspecified. His first recorded case is that of 'The Adventure of the *Gloria Scott*', as recounted to Dr Watson, which took place during the university vacation. Holmes had been developing his powers of observation and deduction and was known amongst fellow students for his singular method of analysing problems. At the time this was nothing more to him than an intellectual exercise. During his work on the *Gloria Scott* mystery, however, it was suggested to him that he would make a brilliant detective and that idea took hold and gave him a direction in life.

Holmes realised that he lacked the broad and varied fields of knowledge which would serve as a foundation for his mental skills. The next few years were dedicated to acquiring that knowledge, and in doing so, he created the man who burst upon the literary scene and met Dr Watson in the first Holmes novel, *A Study in Scarlet*.

In my work, I have suggested that Holmes was at university during the years 1873–75, solving the *Gloria Scott* mystery after his second year. Realising that his particular requirements could not be provided by a university course, he did not return, choosing instead to undertake his own studies. He had boxed and fenced at university and while there is no evidence that he devoted dedicated practice to either later on, it is clear that these were skills he retained. His lodgings in London's Montague Street placed him close to the British Museum where he must have spent many hours studying in the library, and he enrolled at St Bartholomew's Medical College for practical courses in chemistry and anatomy.

And that is where my series begins.

Reviews are so important to authors, and if you enjoyed this novel I would be grateful if you could spare a few minutes to post a review on **Amazon** and **Goodreads**. I love hearing from readers, and you can connect with me online, **on Facebook**, **Twitter**, and **Instagram**.

You can also stay up to date with all my news via **my website** and by signing up to **my newsletter**.

Linda Stratmann

2023

lindastratmann.com

Sapere Books is an exciting new publisher of brilliant fiction and popular history.

To find out more about our latest releases and our monthly bargain books visit our website:
saperebooks.com

Printed in Great Britain
by Amazon